$1-

W9-AUY-029

Running the Dogs

Running the Dogs

Thomas Cochran

FARRAR STRAUS GIROUX

NEW YORK

Distributed in Canada by Douglas & McIntyre Ltd.
Printed in the United States of America
Designed by Barbara Grzeslo
First edition, 2007
1 3 5 7 9 10 8 6 4 2

www.fsgkidsbooks.com

Library of Congress Cataloging-in-Publication Data
Cochran, Thomas, date.
    Running the dogs / Thomas Cochran.— 1st ed.
        p.   cm.
    Summary: When an unexpected snowstorm hits his part of Louisiana, ten-year-old
Tal demonstrates his determination and responsibility after his hunting dogs become
lost in the woods.
    ISBN-13: 978-0-374-36360-4
    ISBN-10: 0-374-36360-9
    [1. Dogs—Fiction. 2. Louisiana—Fiction.] I. Title.

PZ7.C6396 Run 2007
[Fic]—dc22

2006046515

For my parents

Running
the Dogs

I

When Talmidge Cotton heard the forecast on the radio that morning he thought that somebody at the Weather Service must have mixed up the prediction for Louisiana with the one for some northern place like Minnesota, where it would make more sense. Christmas was two days away, and the report said that chances were good for it to be a white one in the northwest corner of the state, which included Tal's town, Oil Camp. Up to six inches of snow were expected to cover the area before the storm ended.

Tal checked the sky (clear) and the temperature (forty-five). The possibility of snow falling on such a day seemed far-fetched. The prediction sounded like some bored weatherman's idea of a practical joke. Half a foot was more than the combined total of snow Tal had seen in his entire life. As a rule, winters in his part of the country were mild, not so very different from the autumns there. Brief cold spells did come and go, and light snow did occasionally dust the ground, but the only real, wonderland-type winter weather he had experienced happened three years before, when he was seven. An ice storm blew into Claiborne Parish and destroyed trees for miles around. One of them was the granddaddy pine that stood in the Cottons' front yard. With a sharp, startling, middle-of-the-night *crack*, the great tree had snapped in two like a stick, providing Tal with one of his most vivid second-grade memories.

Timber was strewn everywhere in the wake of that storm. It lay on roads, in yards, against power lines, and across roofs. Many of the trees that weren't broken were bowed over by the weight that encased them. They looked like ones he and his friends liked to climb and straddle, riding them down and then dismounting to watch as they sprang back upright. These would rise more slowly, if at all. Tal remembered the destruction, but he also remembered the glassy beauty of the ice and the unexpected holiday from school that it gave him.

What fun he'd had on those three dim, bitterly cold days! Daddy made him a sled out of a plank of plywood and some shelf brackets, and Tal spent hour after hour sliding on it while Wink, the dog he had at the time, chased after him. There wasn't anything resembling a hill out where the Cottons lived—two miles north of Oil Camp—but there were places where the land rolled. Still, even where it was flat, as on the road in front of his house, all Tal had to do to go plenty fast was run, dive, and hang on. Sometimes he tried unsuccessfully to ride the sled like a skateboard.

At night, sore from the many hard spills he had taken during the day, he had stood under a hot shower until his chilled skin turned pink and he became drowsy. Then he went to bed early. Hoping that school would remain closed forever, he would burrow cozily beneath his covers and imagine that his bedroom was an igloo set in a stark arctic landscape.

Eventually, of course, the sun returned, the temperature rose, and the ice turned to slush. Soon it disappeared entirely, as dreams do, and people went to work cleaning up the mess. They were at it for several weeks, a period defined for Tal by the incessant, gnawing whine of chain saws.

The winters that had passed since then came and went without producing anything quite as out of the ordinary as the ice storm. Louisiana was just too far south to get any significant winter weather on a regular basis. Except for that annual disappointment, Tal had no complaints about where he lived. Oil Camp was his home, and it probably always would be, as it had been for his parents and theirs before them. He came from a line of people who originally settled the area to work in the oil and gas fields there. The men were roughnecks. They handled drilling pipe on the rigs that dotted the landscape. Later, as the town grew, some of them, like Daddy's father, took other work. He had been a rural mail carrier. Mama's folks were dead and gone now, but Daddy's were still very much a part of Tal's life. They lived in town, over by the football stadium, which was called Roughneck Field.

His grandmother, Mimi, was, in her own words, as healthy as an ox. Unfortunately, the same could not be said about Papa, Tal's grandfather, who had suffered a heart attack back in the spring. He'd recovered nicely from his bypass operation, but he didn't take the kind of care of himself that he was supposed to and lately he'd developed a cough that Tal had seen get away from him more than once. Papa always waved a hand when it did, shrugging it off as nothing more than a little case of what he called the grippe.

"A few spoons of cod-liver oil'll send this foolishness on its way in no time," he said.

Tal knew that this was a bluff, but he also knew that no matter what anybody—including the doctor—thought or said, Papa was going to be Papa. He'd deal with the situation in his own stubborn way. The worst example of this had to do with the pipe that had been his constant companion since he was a young man. Because of his condition, he was under strict orders to give it up. So far he hadn't heeded that advice, although he did claim that he was getting good at not allowing any smoke into his lungs. Everybody in the family wanted him to do more than that and told him so every chance they got. Papa took their preaching about as seriously as he took his cough.

"It ain't really smoking if you don't inhale," he said.

"Why don't you just quit it then?" Daddy said. "Seems to me like you'd have enough sense not to let that get you."

"Yeah," said Jessie, Tal's little sister. "Seems to me like it, too, Papa."

"Y'all don't seem to realize that if this don't get me, something or other's bound to," Papa said. "I rest my case."

"You'll rest more than that when they load you into a box," Mimi said.

"That's the truth," Mama said.

"I believe we're talking about my funeral," Papa said. "And it wouldn't bother me hardly a bit if y'all up and decided to let me enjoy the ride to it."

Tal had heard several such exchanges during the past few months. Papa was hardly feeble, but it was obvious that he wasn't as energetic as he used to be. He'd also lost some weight. Every time Tal saw him light his pipe, he wondered what Papa was trying to prove. But he decided not to pester him. It was clearly a waste of time. Instead, he tried to keep Papa's health at the end of his list of things to think about. This hadn't been hard to do for the past couple of weeks, because the main thing on Tal's mind was Christmas, particularly Christmas night when, if he got his wish, Daddy would finally let him take his dogs into the woods and run them alone, something he'd never done after dark.

Daddy was a foreman on offshore oil rigs in the Gulf of Mexico. He worked a two-week shift every month, overseeing operations on drilling platforms his company owned.

He was scheduled to finish his latest shift at noon the next day, which was Christmas Eve. Then, the company helicopters would fly the workers from the rig to Morgan City, where they'd get into their cars and trucks and go their separate ways. Most of them were from towns in South Louisiana, so they didn't have far to drive. Daddy had over three hundred miles, from the bottom of the state to the top. He didn't care for that part of the job, but the offshore pay was better than he had earned working on inland rigs when he first entered the business. It made the inconvenience of spending half of each month away from his family more than worth his while.

Like Mama and Jessie, Tal missed Daddy badly when he was gone. The two-on, two-off shift was an established and accepted fact of their lives, though, and they were used to the rhythm of it. Once Tal was old enough to understand the schedule, he realized that the two-off part of it was actually to his advantage. During it Daddy always spent quite a bit of time with him. Tal figured that they were together even more than they would have been if Daddy worked nearby and came home every night.

According to the forecast Tal heard that morning, the southern half of the state—from Alexandria on down—was in for some nasty weather, too. Freezing rain was probable, and that was likely to turn to snow before it ended. If this happened, Daddy's return home could be delayed. Tal dismissed this thought as soon as he had it because he didn't believe the prediction in the first place.

Anyone who looked outside that morning would have agreed with him. The forecast really did seem like a mistake. But weather has a mind of its own, and sometimes the people who get paid to guess what it will do are right. Much to Tal's amazement, things began to change as the day progressed. Pushed by a stiff wind, a thick mass of dark clouds formed in the west and spread itself toward the east like a huge quilt, tucking in the sun and covering every speck of blue until the sky was solid gray. By mid-afternoon, the temperature had dropped out of the forties and into the thirties. By dusk, it had reached the twenties, and all of the elements were in place for a considerable winter storm.

2

Daddy called home just after dark. Jessie answered and talked first. Then Mama got on the line. Tal, who had been getting ready to go feed the dogs when the phone rang, waited impatiently for his turn. Seeing how antsy he was, Mama cut her conversation short and handed him the phone.

"Don't hang up," she said. "I'm not through."

"I won't," he said. "Hey, Daddy. Boy, it's looking rough around here. It's serious cold, and the wind's blowing hard enough to rattle the windows."

Daddy laughed.

"Howdy, Tal," he said. "You sound wound up."

"Shoot, who wouldn't be?" Tal said. "It's supposed to snow six inches and looks like it might will. What's it like down yonder?"

"Well, I don't think the Gulf'll freeze, but they're calling for a mess inland and it's getting cold enough to where there might could be one. You ought to hear some of these Cajuns moaning and groaning. They're tough old boys, but this little chilly snap's got them shivering and stomping around like they're on top of Mount Everest. How're the dogs? I bet they're loving this."

"I had them out this afternoon, and they were pretty excited. They're in the pen right now, but I'm fixing to let them loose for a little while after they eat."

"Reckon Mama'll invite them inside for the night?"

Tal could tell that Daddy was smiling when he said it. There was no way Mama would ever let him bring the dogs into the house.

"That'll be the day," Tal said.

"Don't worry," Daddy said. "They'll be fine. You might want to take you an extra blanket out for them, though. They'll appreciate it."

"I got one right here, ready to go."

"Good boy."

"You thought any more about what you promised you would the other day?" Tal said after a brief pause.

"Once or twice," Daddy said.

"And?"

"Oh, like I told you when we talked, we'll just have to see. Okay?"

"I guess so. But keep thinking about it. It's the only thing on my list now, remember."

"Will do, buddy. You take care of Mama and Jessie for me, and tell Mimi and Papa hey if you see them. I'm hoping to be home tomorrow, but I'm not sure what the weatherman's got in store for us. Better put Mama back on before I use up my whole dime here."

Tal said goodbye and returned the phone to Mama. He wished that Daddy had given him more of a hint about what he was thinking, but it had to do with a Christmas present, and Daddy was the kind of person who believed that Christmas presents were for Christmas, not two days before. Plus, if he wasn't seriously considering it, he would have said so on the phone. He would have told Tal to forget the idea and ask for something else. He hadn't, and that was encouraging.

He and Daddy had been at the kitchen table when Tal

first mentioned it to him. Mama had already left for her job answering the phone at City Hall. She liked to say that she and not the mayor was really in charge of Oil Camp because nobody talked to him before talking to her. Jessie was in the front room having her cereal with Daffy Duck, Speedy Gonzales, Foghorn Leghorn, and her special favorite, Wile E. Coyote. Tal usually ate with Jessie and her cartoons on school day mornings, but this was the last chance before Daddy left for offshore to bring up a subject he'd been trying to get the nerve to for quite a while.

"Can I ask you a question, Daddy?" he said.

"You bet," Daddy said.

"Well, it's not exactly a question," Tal said. "It's more like letting you know something."

"I'm listening," Daddy said.

"I want to run the dogs by myself," Tal said. "At night."

He had gone over and over how he would defend this once he said it out loud, carefully planning it so that Daddy would see how reasonable he was. His main argument was that he wasn't asking to hunt alone; that would be foolish because he'd only recently been allowed to use a gun for something other than target practice anyway. All he wanted, he said, was to take the dogs into the woods after dark by himself. Running them, which he and Daddy and some-times Papa did on a regular basis, was mainly just a matter of letting them go and waiting for them to circle back. It was as easy as walking, really.

The only problem would be if they got after a coon be-cause, unlike rabbits and deer, coons refused to turn. They always fled in a straight line until they got tired. Then they simply climbed a tree, leaving the dogs stranded below. And the dogs wouldn't leave a treed coon. You had to go fetch them, and sometimes you had to hike a long way to do it.

"I know my way around out there," Tal said. "It can't be all that much different in the dark. I've been in it with y'all."

"You might be surprised how different the dark is by yourself," Daddy said.

"I'd have my lantern," Tal said. "Like you would, or Papa. I want to be like y'all are."

"Reach me a biscuit, if you would," Daddy said.

Mama had left them a pan of catheads, so named because of their size and shape. Tal passed Daddy one and watched him break and prepare it—butter on one half, cane syrup on the other, a mound of the eggs he'd scrambled on each. He covered both sides with black pepper and stacked them like a sandwich.

"Better let me fix you one," he said.

Tal shook his head. Now that his cards were on the table, he wasn't hungry.

"Your loss," Daddy said, and took a bite.

"We were talking about the dogs," Tal said. "Me running them, I mean."

Daddy swallowed. "I heard you," he said. "That's what we're talking about now. But my guess is that you'll be wanting to hunt with them the day after that."

"No, I won't. I just want to go in with them by myself if they take off like they do sometimes. I think I'm old enough not to have to be with you or Papa."

"I don't mean literally the day after, son. What are you these days, ten?"

"And a half."

"Same difference," Daddy said after a moment. "Ten's ten until it's eleven. I'd rather you be a little older before you go alone. There's plenty of time for you to be like me and Papa."

"You went out with a rifle by yourself when you were eight," Tal said. "Papa told me."

"Papa exaggerates," Daddy said. "I was nine, not that it matters. It was a completely different situation."

Tal rolled his eyes.

"I don't care about hunting by myself yet, Daddy," he said. "I know I'm not ready for that. I just want to run the son-of-a-bitching dogs without anybody else there."

Shocked by the phrase he'd used, he looked back at Daddy and pulled his lips between his teeth as if that might erase it. Papa said it all the time and nobody seemed to mind, but Tal had never cussed in front of Daddy and he knew he'd picked a bad time to start.

For a long moment, the words hung in the air like a noose. Daddy didn't put up with back talk at all, and apologizing for it was a waste of breath so Tal didn't bother. He was out of line and he'd ruined his argument. All he could do was wait and take what came. He listened to the muted noise of Jessie's *Looney Tunes*, wishing he were in there with her.

Daddy drummed his fingers on the table. He had big, powerful hands. Tal watched them, trying not to flinch. Then he let his eyes slide slowly up and noticed that Daddy was nodding his head thoughtfully like he was talking to himself and agreeing with what he said. He even seemed to be trying not to smile.

"Better go rinse your plate and get your teeth brushed," he said. "School bus'll be by directly. Maybe we'll see about letting you take the dogs out for a little nighttime run when I get back."

Tal realized that he'd been holding his breath the entire time since he cussed. He let it out all at once and sucked in a few new ones like he'd just come to the surface after being in deep water.

"You mean it?" he said.

"I mean we'll see," Daddy said.

Tal was so relieved he felt dizzy.

"What do you think I want for Christmas?" he said.

"List I saw the other day had a football on it," Daddy said. "That and a few other items that took up I believe about a page. Why?"

"Because I'm throwing that one away," Tal said. "Just let me run the dogs by myself when it's dark and that's all I want for Christmas this year."

"I'll tell Santa Claus to consider it if I see him," Daddy said.

"That's good enough for me," Tal said.

He picked up his plate and stood looking at Daddy.

"Well?" Daddy said.

"Nothing," Tal said. "I mean, a minute ago? I'm sorry. That kind of just slipped out."

"You been hanging around Papa too much," Daddy said. "Tell Jessie to get herself in gear on your way through. Y'all don't want to miss that bus. I need to pack and get on the road."

Tal realized that something important had happened. He'd said exactly what he thought, and he'd *cussed* doing it. But Daddy let him off without even scolding him. That was a first. Tal felt different and good. It was like he'd taken a step into brand-new territory.

The two weeks that had passed since then seemed even more tedious than they usually did around Christmas. Time dragged, each day somehow managing to move slower than the one before. No matter where he was or what he was doing, all Tal could think about was Christmas night when, he hoped, he'd finally be free to follow his dogs into the woods as far as he dared—just him, all by himself.

He draped the extra blanket on his arm and picked up the bag of chow. Opening the back door, he heard Mama tell Daddy that she was going ahead with Christmas Eve supper as if he would be there. Tal couldn't imagine him missing that, regardless of how bad the weather got.

3

Outside, the wind was making the temperature seem even lower than it actually was. The slim red line of the old Pepsi-Cola thermometer nailed to the side of Daddy's toolshed was just two marks above the 20. Tal looked at it and shivered. He didn't know how to figure the chill factor, but his body told him that it had to be pushing single digits. Next time out, he'd be sure to wear his heavy coat. The jeans jacket he had on was too light for this kind of weather. At least he was wearing gloves.

The wind made a spooky, moaning sound. Tal had heard the same noise somewhere before, but he couldn't quite place it at first. Then he remembered. It was like the air-raid sirens in a documentary Miss Bouchillon had shown the class during history period one day earlier in the year. The movie was about World War II and in it those sirens went off to warn the people of England to take cover whenever they were about to be bombed by German planes.

Leaning into the wind, Tal couldn't help thinking that the sound of the wind might be a kind of warning itself. Tree limbs were flapping up and down like wings, and the power line that ran from the house to the pole that held the yard lamp was whipping back and forth like a jump rope. Tal had never heard of a winter tornado before, but he wouldn't have been too surprised to see a funnel come twisting down out of that dense, dark sky.

The dogs met him at the gate of their pen, greeting him with their usual feeding-time medley of excited whines and yips and barks. All three of them were working their tails so hard that they had to step from side to side to keep themselves facing him. They always did this little jig when they saw him coming, whether he was carrying a bag of food or not. And the feeling was mutual. Regardless of what might be bothering him, the sight of those three beagles never failed to make Tal smile. They were alive in the world, and it was plain that they thought the world was a mighty fine place.

"Y'all hungry, or are you just happy to see me?" he said. "Hang on a second here."

He set the bag and the blanket down and opened the gate. LC and Pete, the two males, immediately shot out of the pen and took off. They stayed side by side, shadows of each other, their noses to the ground. Tal didn't try to stop them because he knew they would start back as soon as they heard the sound of food plinking into their bowls.

Claudia, the female, remained with him. She continued to dance for a moment, then she jumped up and put her forepaws on his leg. The bell on her collar jingled faintly. Tal pulled off his gloves and hunkered down to pet her.

"How's my girl?" he said, stroking her head and back.

Tal dearly loved each of his dogs, but Claudia was his favorite. If anybody had asked him why, he would have had to say that he couldn't explain it any better than he could explain why his favorite color was green or why his favorite food was pork chops. She just was, and he'd known she would be the instant he first saw her.

LC and Pete didn't wait for their supper to be served before circling back to the pen. After a minute or two, here they came, snorting and snuffling and demanding to be rubbed. Tal slid his palms along their sleek flanks, occasionally altering the motion to caress a thin, floppy ear between his thumbs and forefingers. LC moved away from the group and stood beside his bowl. He barked as if to remind Tal of what he was there to do.

"Coming, boss," Tal said.

He gave Claudia and Pete a final stroke apiece and stood. He poured a cup of chow into each of the three bowls, then he stepped back to watch the dogs crunch and snort and either swallow or inhale—it was impossible to tell which—before starting over and doing it again, until they'd consumed every last nugget and were pushing the empty containers around with their noses, their tails lashing contentedly. The way they ate amazed Tal every time he saw it. They always acted like he kept them about half starved.

Pete was the first to realize that he couldn't make any more food appear, followed by LC, then Claudia. Tal had left the gate open for them so they could run around and wear themselves out before having to settle in for the night. One of them would probably find a scent and take off into the woods. They did it all the time. For now he couldn't follow. Daddy said he had to listen from the yard. Tal knew that this was the same as being out there on one level, but on another it was completely different. He thought he was ready to cross the line. Maybe in a couple of nights Daddy would, too.

Because Tal hadn't brought his lantern or turned the yard lamp on, he could barely see what he was doing as he finished his chores. He changed the water in the dogs' trough and hoped it wouldn't freeze during the night. Even if it did, he'd be back out first thing in the morning. They wouldn't die of thirst in a few hours, even though they'd probably act like it. They were characters. Smiling, he shook out their bedding and arranged it, along with the extra blanket, inside the doghouse. He put a handful of food into each of the bowls, then he carried the bag into the yard and listened. The only sound was that constant, sireny wind. After a moment he also noticed the clinking of Mama's chimes, which hung from a facing board above the patio fifty yards or so from where he stood. He wasn't absolutely sure, but he didn't think he'd heard any barking since the dogs left the pen. This was unusual. Normally, one of them would be baying by now. It wasn't anything to worry about, but Tal did wonder why they were being so quiet.

His signal to bring them back was a four-note whistle he'd got from an old black-and-white movie about sailors on the sea. The first and third notes were low, the second and fourth ones high. You held the second longer than the others. Trying it, he discovered that he couldn't whistle at all. His lips were so cold they were numb and uncooperative. They felt like they did after a shot at the dentist's office. He gave up after a couple of attempts and used Daddy's signal, which was simply to call the dogs' names.

"Claudia! Here, Claudia! LC! Come on, LC! Pete! Let's go, Pete!"

He repeated the calls several times, but got no response and blamed the wind. They must have gone into the woods. Or maybe they were ignoring him because they thought he wanted to put them up already, which he didn't. He just wanted to see them, to be in touch. Not hearing them was odd, but there was no reason for him to stand there and freeze while they ran. Wherever they were, they were sure to be having a big time either chasing each other or terrorizing some poor cottontail. All Tal was doing was getting cold, and the smell of woodsmoke had begun to fill the evening air like an invitation. He decided to go warm up for a while and eat a bite of supper. After that he'd dress better and come settle them in for the night. By then, he probably wouldn't even have to whistle. The dogs would be looking for him.

4

Mama was in the front room with Jessie, who was busy examining some of the presents under the Christmas tree, a fragrant cedar that stood against the wall opposite the fireplace. The TV set was tuned to the six o'clock news on Channel 3 out of Shreveport.

"I bet Claudia and them're sure cold," Jessie said.

"I don't know about them, but I'm about half froze," Tal said. "They took off right after they ate. I tried to whistle them back and couldn't even fix my lips right."

"Come thaw yourself out," Mama said.

She was sitting on the stone ledge of the fireplace. Above her, the mantel was decorated with pine boughs, a wooden manger scene Papa had carved when Daddy was little, and a pair of stockings. Jessie's, red with green trim, was hung at one end. Tal's, green with red trim, was at the other.

Mama scooted over and patted the ledge. Tal sat down beside her.

"Were they after something as usual?" she said.

"I couldn't tell," Tal said. "Wind's too loud."

He looked at the TV. A commercial for the Ford place in Minden was on.

"They showed the weather yet?" Tal said.

"It's all they talked about so far," Mama said. "Looks like it might get worse than they were saying earlier, which is hard to believe. I'm sick of hearing about it myself. Cut that off for me, honey."

Jessie punched the TV switch with an oblong package wrapped in plaid paper.

"You figured all your gifts out, Jess?" Tal said.

"This one I have," Jessie said. "It's from Mimi and Papa, and it's going to be my next Barbie. LSU Cheerleader Barbie. I'm opening it tomorrow for my Christmas Eve present."

Jessie collected Barbie dolls. It started when she found

Mama's old ones, including one she called Ghost Barbie because the doll had no head. Tal wasn't sure how many she
had, only that another one arrived just about every time
somebody in the family went to a yard sale.

"Will you make a snowman with me in the morning if
some's really there, Talmidge?" she said.

"We'll roll up a whole family of them if you want to,"
Tal said. "How worse are they saying, Mama?"

"Snow all the way down to DeRidder," Mama said.
"Three to five inches of it that far, six to they're now saying
eight up here. Can you imagine?"

"Not really," Tal said.

"I can," Jessie said. "It'll be like on Christmas cards
with horses and sleighs."

"What about way down like to Morgan City?" Tal said.

"Ice," Mama said.

She and Tal looked at each other long enough for him to
realize that the prediction upset her. Then she turned her
head away and rested her chin on the heel of her hand. For
the first time since he'd heard the original forecast that
morning, Tal realized that there was a very definite possibility that the weather might actually cause Daddy to miss
Christmas Eve and maybe even Christmas itself. Mama was

obviously thinking the same thing, but he went ahead and asked her.

"Will Daddy be stuck?"

Mama answered with a quick shrug of her shoulders.

"How many snow people would be in a family, Talmidge?" Jessie said.

"You tell me," Tal said.

"Four," Jessie said. "I want four like in ours. A daddy and a mama first, then a brother and a sister. That's a family."

"I wish he was already here," Tal said.

"Wish who was?" Jessie said.

Mama stood and walked to the window. She held one of the drapes aside.

"Daddy," Tal said.

"Daddy's coming in tomorrow," Jessie said. "Christmas Eve. He told me he'll be here then, just like Santa Claus."

"Daddy might have to be late, hon," Mama said. "He's way down yonder at his oil rig in the Gulf of Mexico. All of the roads from there to here are fixing to maybe get too icy for him to drive on."

She continued to look out the window, her back to Tal and Jessie.

"He could just catch him a ride with Santa then," Jessie said.

Tal knew who Santa really was, but Jessie was only six and didn't. She was still a couple of years away from even being suspicious about him.

"Santa can't give rides," Tal said. "His sleigh's too full for there to be room."

"Like at the end," Jessie said.

"What?" Tal said.

"Where Jesus's mama and daddy went to have him born," Jessie said. "They had to go out with the cows be-cause there wasn't room at the end."

"You mean the inn," Tal said. "Like where we stayed at in Florida that vacation. Days Inn. I-n-n."

"Was the Gulf of Mexico we went in the same one where Daddy is?" Jessie said.

"There's only one," Tal said.

"But ours didn't have any oil wells in it," Jessie said.

"You just couldn't see them," Tal said. "The Gulf's big, like an ocean."

"And scary," Jessie said. "Daddy said there were sharks and stingrays, but I only saw one little jellyfish."

Tal poked the fire, coaxing a new flame that moved

across one of the logs like a wave. Jessie began repositioning the packages under the tree. She knew exactly how many there were and could say which person they belonged to without looking at the tags. As she worked, she hummed bits and pieces of little-kid Christmas songs. Tal recognized "Frosty the Snowman," and the one about reindeer paws up on the roof. Jessie wasn't going to let anything get in the way of her excitement about the holiday, but Tal felt his own beginning to dwindle.

"Come see, y'all," Mama said.

She pulled the cord and parted the drapes. Jessie was at the window before Tal could stand.

"Hurry, Talmidge," she said. "Look at all the flakes, Mama!"

Blown by the wind, they came down more sideways than straight. And they were huge, at least the size of quarters. The first ones melted when they hit the ground, but there were so many of them that they soon began to build up on each other. The yard and the road in front of the house were changing from dark to light like magic.

"Well, here it is," Mama said. "It's so pretty I almost don't even hate what it means."

Tal watched the snow. If Daddy hadn't been away, he

would have thought that being this close to a genuine white Christmas was ideal. It almost was anyway. He and Jessie could build as many snowmen as they wanted. They could take turns on the sled Daddy had made after the ice storm. They could have snowball fights. Better yet, he could get together with his friends and have a snowball war. They could play football, too, tackle football in the snow.

But having snow on the ground was one thing, and having your father home for Christmas was another. Given the choice, Tal knew that he'd pick Daddy in half a second, even if it meant trading his first white Christmas for another shorts-and-T-shirts one like last year's. Still, Mama was right. The falling snow sure was a pretty sight to see.

5

Cooking was Mama's hobby and she was good at it. Daddy kept her freezer stocked with fish year-round. During hunting season he supplied a variety of game as well. The previous fall, Tal—who had been a fisherman ever since he could remember—was allowed to hunt with Daddy for the first time. The rifle he carried was a bolt-action, single-shot .22 Winchester that originally belonged to Papa. Tal quickly proved himself to be steady and accurate with it.

Following Daddy's example, he deeply respected the woods and the creatures there and took no particular pleasure from the actual killing he did. In fact, like all true hunters, he always felt a moment of intense sadness when he brought an animal down. But providing meat for Mama to cook was the reason they hunted, and Tal felt no remorse at all when he sat down to one of her fine meals. She fried, baked, or stewed the rabbits he and Daddy bagged. The squirrels they came home with became the main ingredient in her spicy mulligan. Except for pork chops, which remained at the top of Tal's list of favorites, nothing from the grocery store could compare with the game he helped furnish. Someday that would include venison.

Because she would be working in the kitchen most of the next day preparing the family's Christmas Eve supper, Mama had taken a shortcut that night, reheating a pot of leftover beans and rice. Tal was the only one who ate any. Mama said she had no appetite, and Jessie wanted a peanut butter sandwich instead.

"When're you going to call Claudia and them in, Talmidge?" she said.

"Soon's I finish these vittles."

Jessie pinched her nose and made a face.

"Ew," she said. "Vittles is what Papa called it when I spent the night and he put squirrel brains in his eggs at breakfast. He said, 'You better have some of these vittles, kid. They're larapin.' But I told him I'd never eat a vittles if that's what it is."

"It don't just mean squirrel brains in your eggs," Tal said. "Vittles is any food."

"Is it, Mama?" Jessie said.

Mama nodded.

"Then I must be having me a peanut butter sandwich vittles," Jessie said.

Tal almost choked trying not to laugh before he could swallow the bite he'd just taken. Mama got tickled, too.

"What, y'all?" Jessie said.

"Oh, just thanks for being such a treasure," Mama said.

She walked over and hugged Jessie's neck.

"Peanut butter sandwich vittles," Tal said. "You're something else, Jess."

Jessie said she wanted to go outside with Tal after supper, but Mama told her she didn't think so. Jessie folded her arms and wondered how come.

"It wouldn't be too fun right now," Tal said. "The wind'll practically blow you over. Plus, it's freezing enough without that. It'll be better in the morning when it's light."

Actually, he just didn't want to have to keep an eye on her.

"Tal's right, honey," Mama said. "You need to wait and go out tomorrow."

"I'll be glad when I'm ten and grown up," Jessie said. "Then I can go anywhere whenever I want to."

"You still have to ask," Tal said. "Believe me."

"Maybe I won't do it," Jessie said.

"You better," Mama said.

She opened a cabinet and took out a bottle of vanilla.

"How would y'all like some snow ice cream later?" she said. "I saw a recipe for it in a magazine the other day, and I'd like to give it a try now that I've got the chance. We'll have us a taste with hot chocolate."

Jessie clapped her hands.

"Dessert vittles," she said. "Yummy. I'll help."

"You don't have to say whatever it is and then 'vittles' next," Tal said. "All food is vittles."

Jessie checked to make sure that Mama wasn't looking, then she showed Tal her tongue. He gave her a fake smile. She was still pouting because he was going out and she couldn't. He was relieved not to have to deal with her, but he did understand how she felt. It wasn't easy being a little kid waiting your turn to do things you wished you could do right then.

"Good supper, Mama," he said. "I guess I'll go see what the hounds are up to."

"Thank you, son," she said. "Sorry it was just leftovers, but I'll make up for it tomorrow evening. Promise. Be sure to bundle up."

"After a while ago, I'm putting on every warm thing I have," Tal said.

6

A good inch of snow already covered the ground, and it continued to fall in the same huge flakes they'd watched earlier. Amazingly, the temperature seemed to have dropped several more degrees. It was getting down below anything Tal had ever felt. Still stiff, the wind caused his eyes to water. But that was fine. The weather was strange and wonderful, and he was happy to have it all to himself.

He expected the dogs to show up at any moment, so he didn't signal them. He made a couple of snowballs and tossed them at the toolshed. Both of them came apart before they reached their target. The snow was too dry to stay together. It wasn't at all like the wet, slushy kind he'd seen in the past, the kind you could grab a handful of, press together as hard as a baseball, and throw a mile. This wouldn't pack at all. It was the real winter thing, light and powdery. It reminded Tal of sand.

Facing the woods, he stood and listened for a moment. He didn't hear the dogs. Instead of worrying about that, he fell over backwards and fanned his arms to make a snow angel. Then he rolled over and over. When he stopped, he lay on his back and caught flakes with his tongue. His head was spinning, a sensation he enjoyed.

Tal loved being outside and always had. Daddy made sure of that. He had introduced Tal to the outdoors early on. First, he taught him how to catch and clean fish. Later, he taught him how to find his way around in the thick pine woods that surrounded the Cottons' house. Those woods soon became Tal's main playground. There was no place he would rather be.

When the dogs were about eight months old, he and Daddy began running them at night. Papa often joined them back then, but he'd only gone a couple of times since his heart attack. Tal missed having him there because he always had a story or two to tell while they waited for LC, Pete, and Claudia to make their circle and return.

The beagles had worked well together from the start. They were just shy of being two years old now, but their pattern was the same as it had been when they were puppies. Regardless of which one got the initial scent, the other two would immediately join the chase and help force whatever they were after into tighter and tighter turns until they had it headed directly toward Tal and Daddy. The strategy was ideal for rabbits, which they were bred to hunt, but it also worked on the occasional deer. Being climbers, coons didn't need to turn. And because the dogs weren't picky about their quarry, they often jumped one and wound up baying below a tree deep in the woods. Daddy didn't like having to go fetch them, but Tal didn't mind because it allowed him to stay up that much later.

Pete's voice was the highest pitched, LC's the lowest. Claudia's split the difference and was to Tal's ear the finest of the three. Hearing all of them together was his favorite sound in the world. It must have seemed like murder to a rabbit, but Tal heard it as pure beauty.

"Listen at that," Daddy had said the first time it happened. "I don't think there's anything much prettier to hear than beagles on the trail."

Papa had been with them that night.

"I'll take it over a symphony orchestra any time myself," he said. "Not that I wouldn't take just about anything over a symphony orchestra, but y'all know what I mean."

Tal had goose bumps.

"It's like bells," he said.

Because he associated the dogs' voices in full cry with the ringing of bells, he'd attached a marble-sized one to each of their collars. LC's and Pete's came off and were lost after a short time, but Claudia's stayed in place. This seemed appropriate to Tal because Claudia was clearly the leader of the little pack. More often than not, she was the first to find a scent. LC and Pete had their moments, but they usually wound up following their sister.

Tal himself followed Daddy. During their initial nighttime outings, moving around in the dark woods spooked him, so he always stayed as close to his father as a shadow. When Daddy paused, Tal paused. When Daddy walked, Tal walked. Trying not to pay any attention to the tricks his mind played on him, he kept his eyes on the ground ahead of him and held his lantern so that its light combined with

Daddy's to create a visible path. Still, the illuminated area never seemed quite large enough. The lanterns were able to push back only a few feet of darkness at a time. The rest of the woods remained inky black and threatening.

As time passed, he began to give Daddy more and more room. He marked him as intently as ever, but he did so from farther and farther away, gradually increasing the distance between them until finally he saw only the light from the other lantern moving through the trees. Eventually, he was able to let it out of his sight entirely. Once he could do that, he started wondering what it would be like to run the dogs on his own. Being out there with Daddy was a major reason he enjoyed running them so much, but Daddy was always in charge. Tal thought he'd like having that responsibility all to himself once in a while. He didn't doubt that he could handle it. He just needed permission. Now that he had finally asked for it, he was more hopeful than ever that he would be successful.

"Tal!"

It was Mama calling from the back door. Sitting up, he turned his head and saw her standing there, a silhouette.

"Talmidge!"

He didn't respond. The yard lamp came on. Mama

stepped out onto the patio. She put her hand to her forehead like a visor.

"Talmidge Cotton!"

"Here, Mama," he said. "I'm right here."

"Lordamercy, son," Mama said. "What are you doing down on the ground?"

"There's snow on it, Mama," Tal said.

"I can see that," Mama said.

She knelt and swept some snow into a mixing bowl.

"Brr, it's cold," she said. "Hurry up and get the dogs called, Talmidge. You're fixing to be sick as a mule."

"I bet a little snow wouldn't make a mule sick, Mama," Tal said.

"Maybe not," she said. "But a mule would probably have the good sense to stay up off of it, unlike at least one boy I know."

She opened the back door.

"Ten minutes, Tal," she said. "Get the dogs in and come on inside."

"On my way," Tal said.

He took another roll in the snow after Mama shut the door.

7

Tal stood and brushed himself off. He realized that he still hadn't heard the dogs, and their silence now made him a little uneasy. Walking slowly, like an Indian scout, he moved to the side of the house hoping to find them over by the dryer vent, where they liked to go when it was cold. He wondered how close he could get before one of them noticed him. Probably not very, he thought.

Sure enough, Mama had a load of clothes drying. The steam coming through the vent made the house look like an enormous, idling vehicle, but the smell of it was clean. It combined with the woodsmoke to sweeten the frigid air. Tal crept forward.

Disappointed that the dogs were not there, he returned to the backyard and stopped between the pen and the woods. Normally a black wall at that hour, the first line of trees had taken on a coat of snow and appeared as a massive set of lacy white curtains. Tal tried to see past it but couldn't. He whistled and listened. Only the wind answered, that and Mama's chimes.

Trying to block those sounds from his mind, he stepped to the edge of the yard, framed his mouth with his hands, and called the dogs' names. He wished his voice was as strong as Daddy's because the dogs always heard Daddy when he called them. He tried again. There was no response.

He suddenly became aware of how cold he was. The weather no longer seemed wonderful to him. It just seemed strange, and he didn't like his dogs being out there in it. He considered a couple of possibilities. What if they'd treed a coon and were a mile away, waiting to be fetched? What if the wind, the cold, and the snow had confused them and caused them to run too far beyond the tree line to find their way back? The first was more likely than the second, but there was nothing he could do in either case because now that it was dark, he wasn't allowed to go past where he was standing.

Swallowing hard, he pictured the dogs and let his mind drift back to the sequence of events that led to his getting them. It all started with Wink's death. Tal had seen that happen, and it was one of his worst memories. The two of them were in a ditch half a mile or so up the road from the Cottons' house. It was a warm spring day, the first clear one after a week of rain. Ankle-deep water stood in the ditch. Tal was catching crawdads in a coffee can while Wink explored a few yards away. Tal wasn't paying attention to the dog, but when he heard Wink growl and then start barking frantically he looked to see what was the matter. The hair on Wink's back was up, and his voice sounded wrong.

"Come here, Wink," Tal said, slapping his thigh. "It's okay, boy."

He was about to take a step forward when the moccasin struck. It hit the dog twice—once on his nose and once on his left eye—so fast that Tal didn't even realize what had happened until it was over and Wink, yelping in pain, was running past him.

Tal couldn't see the snake, but he knew it was right

there. He was afraid to move. Except for the coffee can, he didn't have anything to defend himself with if the moccasin decided to come after him, too, so he froze. His heart was racing, and he was having a hard time keeping himself from screaming. He didn't mind snakes in general, but he hated moccasins. They were aggressive and unpredictable. He wondered if this one was watching him, ready to strike again.

The thought of it was too much. With a shout like karate fighters make before they break boards, he dropped the coffee can and jumped out of the ditch. Keeping his eye on the spot where he thought the snake was, he backed slowly away. Then he turned and ran to the house to check on Wink.

He found him under the toolshed, poisoned and struggling. Wink wasn't a big dog, and the venom moved quickly through his system. Tal tried to coax him out but couldn't. All he could do was watch his friend vomit and jerk and try to breathe. Daddy wasn't there to put him out of his misery, and this was before Tal knew how to use a gun. Even if he had known, he wouldn't have been able to, because Daddy always unloaded all of his weapons and locked them in a cabinet before he left for the Gulf. Tal felt completely helpless.

He spent a good deal of time in the days immediately following Wink's death trying to decide whether he wanted another dog or not. He mentioned this to Daddy on the phone, and Daddy said he understood. Tal didn't think he did, though, not really. How could anybody who hadn't been there to see it understand the pain of losing Wink in such an awful way? How could anybody who didn't have to dig a hole and put something he loved in it forever possibly know the feeling?

Dogs, he'd thought, reviewing what happened to the four he had known—all they do in the end is get sick with heartworms, like Boone, or run over, like Rags and Shorty, or bit by a snake, like Wink. You have them for a while, then they're gone. No matter how much you love them, you always lose them. You can't escape that because sooner or later it's going to happen. Eventually, he decided that Wink was going to be his last dog for the simple reason that if he didn't get another one he wouldn't have to go through losing one ever again.

By the time Daddy's shift in the Gulf was over, Tal's

grief had loosened its grip on him, but he remained convinced that not replacing Wink was the right thing to do. Daddy listened to this news without interrupting. There was a long pause before he responded.

"I must have had a dozen dogs die on me in my life," he said. "And I do see your point about it being hard, son. It is, every single time. It makes you sad and mad and hurt, all at once. You hate it because, like you just said, you tend to forget the good part of having them and get stuck on the bad, the ending. It passes, though. I promise you that. Then you kind of forget it and go back to better memories."

"I don't guess I'll ever do that with Wink if I live to be the oldest man in the world," Tal said.

"My bet is that you will," Daddy said. "Give it some time. It'll fade. After a while you'll start remembering how much you like having a dog around the house. By the way, I've told you about my old buddy Claude Thaxton, haven't I?"

"From the job?" Tal said.

Daddy nodded.

"Thax used to be my best friend out there," he said. "I wish he was still with us because he's a card. Anyway, he made me an offer one time I never thought I'd take him up on until you said what you said on the phone the other evening. I gave him a call right after that. Told him about Wink and asked him if his offer still stood."

"What was it?" Tal said.

"Well, it has to do with dogs," Daddy said. "Thaxton raises them. That's about all he ever talked about out on the rig because he was wanting to quit roughnecking and start himself a kennel. He'd say, 'It's my destiny, Cotton, the raising of beagles is.' I mean, he'd go on about it until you weren't hardly hearing him anymore. 'The beagle is the perfect dog. Just the right size, good pet, good hunter, loyal, true, dependable as sunrise, sounds like a million bucks on the trail,' and so forth and so on. Thax'd worry the rear end off a brass monkey listing the virtues of beagles."

"Did he start his kennel?" Tal said.

"Finally did it," Daddy said. "It was a sideline for him at first, but it grew into a full-time occupation, which is why he left the company."

Tal had begun to suspect where this was heading, and he was surprised to find himself getting excited about it.

"What'd he offer you?" he said.

Daddy smiled.

"What he offered me was the pick of a litter, free of

charge, whenever I said the word. Now, I may be getting ahead of myself here, given what you been saying about how you feel, but I been thinking this might be a good time to go take a look at old Thax's hounds, which is what I told him on the telephone. He said, 'Well, Cotton, you just load up and roll on over here soon as you get the go-'head from that boy of yours. I got me some dandies that are weaned and ready to light out on their own.' I don't know, though. I guess it depends on how a beagle pup sounds to you, Talmidge. What do you say?"

For a moment, Tal felt like he was standing on a plat-form above a pool of water that he knew was freezing cold. He needed to either dive on in and get used to it or turn away and wonder what he'd missed. It wasn't an easy choice to make, but there it was—now or never—and Daddy was waiting. Tal took a deep breath. He had to dive.

"It sounds pretty good," he said.

The two of them drove over to Elysian Fields, Texas, the following Saturday, which was as fine a day as Tal could have dreamed. It was late May, school was nearly out, and he was on his way to pick out a new puppy, something he'd never done. In the past, Daddy had always chosen the Cot-tons' dogs, and he liked grown ones.

The kennel was just south of Elysian Fields, which was almost as close to the Louisiana line in east Texas as Oil Camp was to the Arkansas line in northwest Louisiana. The trip lasted only a couple of hours, but when they arrived Tal felt like he had been riding all day. He was anxious to deal with the business at hand.

Claude Thaxton greeted them as they were getting out of the truck. He was the tallest person Tal had actually stood next to. Daddy wasn't short, but Thaxton had him beat by a head, not even counting the immense cowboy hat he wore. Tal felt like he'd shrunk. Thaxton shook his hand and told him it was a pleasure to welcome him to Texas. Tal said it was a pleasure to be there and figured that Thaxton's massive hand would have made about four of his.

"Well, all right," Thaxton said. "Now, there's no use arguing about this, Cotton, so don't even bother to commence, but I got a couple of beasts I want y'all to take a gander at. I say 'a couple' because I done decided it'd be a shame not to send them off together."

Tal looked at Daddy, expecting him to tell Thaxton that he thanked him kindly but one would have to do. Daddy just shook his head.

"You Texans always think big, don't you?" he said.

"Only way to think," Thaxton said. "Big is good, and two'll double your fun."

He led them to a pen that had three pups in it.

"Them two's male, LC and Pete," he said. "The runt there's female, unchristened."

The males were practically identical. They had black coats and tails with brown tips, white legs and undersides, black ears, and brown faces.

"Good-looking dogs," Daddy said.

Tal thought so, too, but he couldn't keep his eyes off the runt. She was marked exactly like the males, with two exceptions: her tail was white-tipped and her face was bisected by a black streak that dropped from her crown and ran the length of her snout. Tal wouldn't have changed a thing about her. She was absolutely beautiful to him.

"Why's the little one not named?" he said.

"No reason," Thaxton said. "Tell the truth, I've just been calling the males LC and Pete after a couple of old boys in town. Names seem to go together. I don't even know what LC stands for, come to think of it. You take them, you can call them anything you want."

He opened the pen. Tal stepped inside and picked the female up. She sniffed him, then she began licking his face.

"I like you, too," he said. "Hey, girl."

"Oh, Lord," Thaxton said. "Looks like we might have us a little love affair on our hands here, Cotton."

"Could be," Daddy said.

LC and Pete were competing for Tal's attention, yapping and nipping at the cuffs of his jeans. Cradling the female in one arm like a football, he sat down to pet the males. They rolled onto their backs, and he rubbed their tight bellies.

"LC," he said. "Pete. And you, whoever you are."

Tracing their faces, he discovered that their teeth were tiny but sharp.

"Whoa!" he said. "I ain't dinner."

He wanted to ask Daddy if they could take all three of them, but he didn't. There wasn't any sense in ruining a good moment with a foolish question.

"Offer stands, by the way, Cotton," Thaxton said. "Zero down on a zero loan with zero interest, no matter how many you take."

"Hard to argue with that," Daddy said. "I don't know, though. I drove over here thinking one, and here I am halfway talked into two. Tal yonder looks like he wouldn't argue too hard against it. Three's a stretch."

Tal continued playing with the puppies. They were like three live balls bouncing and rolling around. He pretended not to be listening to the men, but he was hanging on to their every word.

"Three's also company," Thaxton said. "And them three's yours for the asking."

Completely smitten, Tal didn't believe he could stand to leave any of them behind. He gathered the three pups together.

"What do you think, son?" Daddy asked. "Reckon you could handle three?"

Tal hugged the dogs tighter.

"I don't doubt it a bit," Thaxton said.

Daddy scratched his head. He looked down, then he looked up.

"I don't suppose I do either," he said.

Until that moment, Tal had never understood how come people sometimes cried when they were happy.

"I do know somebody's mama who's fixing to have a walleyed fit when we get back to the house," Daddy said. "Not to mention somebody's wife."

"She'll get over it," Thaxton said. "Won't she, Talmidge?"

"I guess she'll have to," Tal said.

Thaxton pushed his hat back on his head and whooped.

"I swear, Thax, you could sell steak to a vegetarian," Daddy said.

"He'd thank me for it, too," Thaxton said.

And so it was done. After thinking that he'd never get involved with another dog, Tal was the proud owner of three. LC, Pete, and Claudia. He named the little female in honor of Claude Thaxton.

Mama did have a fit when they arrived home, but it wasn't much of one. The beagles made quick work of winning her and Jessie's favor, though Mama put her foot down about where they were going to live.

"Outside," she said. "Starting tonight. If you want inside dogs, you get poodles or Chihuahuas, not beagles."

"But they are just babies," Jessie said.

"Baby hound dogs," Mama said. "End of discussion."

Because they were puppies and because Tal wanted to minimize the hazards they would face outside, Daddy agreed to the idea of building them a pen. It was ready in a few days. Tal helped with some of the construction, but his main task was to keep the pups out from underfoot while Daddy poured and smoothed the concrete, stretched and secured the fencing, and sawed and nailed the wood for their house.

Because Mama wouldn't let them inside, the dogs spent the nights before the pen was finished in the toolshed. Tal stayed with them, using an old cot for a bed. They started out on a pile of towels inside a peach crate, but they somehow always managed to wind up with him on the cot before morning. He got so used to the arrangement that he didn't want it to end. Once it did, the dogs missed his presence as much as he missed theirs. Lying in his own bed, he could hear them whining through his open window.

"They'll get adjusted," Daddy said. "Just be patient."

There was nothing that Tal didn't love about his dogs. They became his constant companions, his best friends. They were always ready to play, but what they seemed to enjoy most was going to work in the woods.

"That's because they're hunters," Daddy said. "Their purpose in life, bottom line, is to put their noses to the ground, find game, and deliver it to you."

Since he'd had them, Tal had rarely gone to sleep without knowing where his dogs were. They would often leave the yard after their evening feeding, but they usually came in before he went to bed. Never once had they failed to return by morning. Now, standing there in the freezing cold with heavy snow falling, he had a bad feeling. The idea that they might have gotten lost entered his mind again. This time it caused his throat to tighten.

He shook his head and told himself to hush. LC, Pete, and Claudia deserved more credit than he was giving them. They could handle a little winter weather. But the situation still made him anxious. It was a strange night, and he knew that what he was thinking might be true.

8

The light from the yard lamp reached almost to the dogs' pen, which in daytime was visible from the window above the kitchen sink. Tal pulled a stool over there and set up his watch. Mama and Jessie were having their snow ice cream and hot chocolate—their dessert vittles—in the front room by the fire. Tal's bowl and cup sat untouched on the counter, the ice cream now melted and the chocolate gone cold.

He kept his eyes on the yard. He couldn't see well because of the falling snow, but he thought that if he looked hard enough the familiar shapes of LC, Pete, and Claudia would eventually materialize. It didn't seem possible to him that they might not. He watched the yard as intently as any sailor ever watched the horizon in search of land. When it was Jessie's bedtime, Mama called him to come tell his sister good night. He left his spot reluctantly.

"Are the dogs lost, Talmidge?" Jessie said. "Mama says they might be, and I don't want them to."

"I know," Tal said. "Me neither. Maybe for a while they are. But they'll come back. You'll see."

Mama was watching them from the doorway. "Tell Tal night-night so I can tuck you in," she said.

"Night-night, Talmidge," Jessie said. "See you in the morning."

"Okay," Tal said. "Night, Jess."

He started toward the door.

"Talmidge?" Jessie's voice stopped him.

"What?"

"Tell Claudia and them night-night for me when they get home."

"Will do," Tal said.

Mama came into the kitchen a few minutes later. She was carrying Tal's pillow and a blanket.

"I kind of figured you'd be sleeping in here," she said.

"I ain't sleeping nowhere if I can help it," Tal said.

"These are just in case," Mama said. "You might as well be half comfortable."

She laid the pillow on the counter and placed the blanket on Tal's shoulders like a cape. It was made of flannel cloth and had the same picture of a hunter and a pair of pointers stamped on it in a repeating pattern. It smelled like the cedar chest where it was kept. Still looking out the window, Tal wrapped the blanket around himself. Mama stood behind him and rubbed his neck.

"You want me to heat that chocolate back up for you?" she said.

Tal shook his head. Mama began to massage his shoulders.

"If they aren't back by morning, you probably ought to call Papa and y'all go look for them together," she said. "He'll carry you around in his pickup."

"If he feels like it," Tal said. "I'd go out there right now if I could."

"I know you would, sweetie, but you can't and it's too late and stormy even if you could. Daddy'd skin you and me both if you did and he found out."

Tal didn't respond. Mama stopped massaging him.

"Hear me, Talmidge?" she said. "I'm serious now. Do not leave this house."

"Yessum," Tal said. "I hear you."

She resumed kneading his shoulders.

"Daddy's going to call first thing to let us know what he thinks about the roads. I s'pect he'll have to wait a day, but we'll just have to see. Surely he can get out of there and be here Christmas night."

"It might be seventy by then. You know what, Mama?"

"What, hon?"

"I'm starting to really get worried. It's different out there tonight."

"I know it. The only thing I can tell you is that they're bound to be fine. They're sturdy and smart. They've always come back before. Don't forget that."

"But it's cold and all that snow. I never should've let them loose."

"Don't say that. They have each other. They'll stay as warm as they can."

"That's what I'm trying to hope."

Mama kissed the top of Tal's head.

"This sure has been an odd day," she said. "If you're

okay, I think I'm fixing to go take my bath and call it done. I'll cut the lights out on my way through."

She kissed the top of his head again and squeezed his shoulders a final time.

"I liked that, Mama," he said.

"Good luck," she said. "Don't go blind looking."

Tal thought that he'd be able to stare out the window all night if he had to, but he nodded off into a dreamless sleep before Mama even finished running her bathwater. He knew this because when he woke up that was the last sound he remembered hearing. Snow was still falling, though not as heavily as it had been. It was coming almost straight down. The wind had calmed.

Slightly disoriented, Tal checked the clock on the oven. It was nearly midnight. He wasn't sure what time Mama went to bed, but it had to have been before eleven. He'd slept for at least an hour. What if the dogs had come home and he'd missed them? Their gate was open, so they could easily have returned and gone into their house.

He peered through the window. Mama had left the yard lamp on. He studied the outline of the pen. The doghouse itself was completely shadowed, invisible. He didn't allow himself to get his hopes up. There was only a slight chance that they were in it, but he wanted to know for sure. He *had* to. Moving quickly, he bundled up again, grabbed his lantern and a book of matches, and slipped out the back door, opening and pulling it to as quietly as he could.

The air was a shock. He'd gotten so warm wrapped up in the blanket that he was immediately uncomfortable. He started to look at the thermometer on the toolshed but decided not to because he didn't need to see the actual number. It was cold enough. His pants felt like they were stuck to his legs. At least the wind had let up. The only sound he could hear other than his own breathing, which was audible because his ears were covered by a stocking cap, was the squeaking of his boots as he walked toward the pen. Thick clouds were riding so low in the sky that the whiteness of the fallen snow reflected off of them. The night glowed eerily.

He knew before he looked into it that the doghouse was empty. Seeing the untouched bedding made him feel even colder. He shivered. The dogs were still out there somewhere, lost or hurt or both. He stared at the place he had fixed for them, the place where they should have been. It looked wrong to him. He already knew what he was going to do.

Tal wasn't in the habit of disobeying Daddy and Mama, but Mama was asleep and Daddy was far away. Even if they found out, surely they'd understand that he had a good reason for breaking their rules. He wasn't doing anything against them. He was doing something for his dogs. It was his fault that they were gone. He owed them a search.

He took several steadying breaths and told himself that there was nothing to be afraid of. He was as ready as he ever would be. If he got in trouble, he got in trouble. He didn't care about that anyway. All he cared about was finding his dogs, which he definitely wasn't going to do by looking out the kitchen window. His mind was made up. Before he could change it, he lit the lantern, adjusted the wick, and headed for the woods.

9

The Cottons' house faced Thousand Pines Road, which met Highway 79 a mile to the east. There were some open pastures in the area that surrounded Oil Camp, but the majority of the land was covered with thick stands of pines crisscrossed by a confusing network of dirt roads and two-tracks. Some of these led to sites where oil or gas wells worked or once had. Others led to clearings left by loggers. The rest no longer led anywhere. They just gradually faded into a tangle of underbrush.

Tal had a fairly good sense of direction, but he was a poor judge of time. He wished he'd thought to bring along a watch. Without one he was going to have to estimate how long he stayed gone. He decided to try for an hour, thirty minutes in and thirty minutes out. If he didn't have any luck by then, he could at least say that he'd taken a decent shot.

Once he moved into the woods, he realized that the snow wasn't as deep because the trees had caught a lot of it. He wondered if any of them would break like so many had after the ice storm. It seemed likely. All around him, limbs were sagging under the weight that was on them. Some of the smaller trees looked like half-closed umbrellas.

He reached an open place after a few minutes of winding his way through the trunks. He'd been walking due south. Now he turned west. When he and Daddy ran the dogs, they tried to keep them as far away from Highway 79 as possible, so they might have gone in this direction out of habit. But there was no telling for certain what they'd done. They could have crossed Thousand Pines Road headed north toward Arkansas as far as Tal knew.

The opening was a two-track, just wide enough for one vehicle. Tal stopped and gave his signal whistle. The sound of it seemed extra loud in the hushed woods, but he wasn't sure that it carried. If it did, it wasn't far enough to get an answer from the dogs. He wondered how many other animals heard it—rabbits and squirrels, coons and deer, possums and birds, and things he didn't care to think about. Nothing stirred, but he knew that countless pairs of eyes were bound to be watching him. This reminded him that he was by himself in the dark woods for the first time in his life.

The snow was deeper on the two-track than it had been in the woods, and more of it was coming down. To keep a steady pace, he had to pick up his feet like he was marching. He wasn't cold anymore, but he was beginning to feel discouraged. When he left the house, he thought that if he didn't immediately find the dogs they would immediately find him. He thought they would somehow sense his presence.

Although he didn't want to admit it to himself, he was also becoming apprehensive. This surprised and embarrassed him because he thought he'd outgrown it. The last time the woods frightened him had happened so long ago that he could barely remember it. The sensation was familiar, though. It was like a dream where you were being followed by something that moved when you moved and stopped when you stopped. You couldn't see or define it, but you knew it was there and that it was against you.

Tal held the lantern head-high and watched the shadows

the light created. The trees and the undergrowth on either side of the opening seemed to come alive. They loomed like tidal waves poised to close over and smother him. He would have given anything to see the light from Daddy's lantern moving through the trees. Feeling small and alone, he began to sing.

"God rest ye, merry gentlemen, let nothing you dismay."

Years ago, when he learned the song, he misunderstood those last two words as a name. Judas May. He knew who Judas Iscariot was, but he'd never heard of Judas May. He asked Mama and Daddy about it. After they finished laughing, they explained the mistake and the meaning of *dismay*. Mama said it was to be upset. Daddy said it was more than that.

"It's to be afraid," he said.

Tal sang louder.

"Oh-wo ti-i-dings of co-om-fort and joy . . ."

His voice sounded thin to him. It had no strength in it. His throat was strangling the words. Not only was he by himself in the woods for the first time, he was also there without anybody knowing it. He was literally cut off from the rest of the world. Other than himself, there wasn't a single person who could say where Talmidge Cotton was at that moment.

He tried to continue the song, but he forgot the next line. He fought to keep himself from losing his nerve entirely by repeating what he'd already sung. But this only reminded him of how alone he was. He stopped walking and listened. He was thoroughly spooked now. Awful shadows surrounded him. He thought he might have heard something, but he wasn't sure if he had or if his mind was just playing tricks on him the way it used to. There was a roaring sound in his ears, then something else—a crash so loud and abrupt and nearby that he didn't hear it so much as he felt it.

Startled into motion, he turned and ran. His legs felt heavy and out of control. They buckled under him as in a nightmare, but he remained upright long enough to leave the two-track and stumble a few yards into the woods, where he tripped and lost his grip on the lantern. It flew out of his hand. The glass shattered, and the light was instantly extinguished by the snow.

Tal scrambled to his feet. Now the trees themselves were shadows. Their low branches slapped him as he ran. He ducked his head, but a rough limb raked him just below his left eye. He put up his hands and staggered blindly through the maze of trunks and branches, the tangle of brush. He stumbled and fell several more times, but he didn't stay down any longer than it took him to hit the ground and lift himself from it. His heart was racing and his breathing was ragged. He pushed himself to keep going. He thought he was running for his life.

At last he saw the yard lamp. It glowed like a beacon. He moved toward it. He was almost home, almost safe. Using the last bit of his energy, he sprinted out of the woods and into his backyard. He fell face-first into the snow. He was breathing hard. The cold air burned his throat and lungs. He spat. He thought he might vomit.

He lay there for a long time before standing. The sick feeling passed. His breathing steadied. He kicked disgustedly at the snow. He walked to the dogs' pen and leaned against it, unable to believe how quickly he had surrendered. He thought he was ready to enter the woods alone, but he wasn't. He thought of the story his family might have told when he was older and forgiven. Remember the Christmas it snowed and the dogs got lost? Remember how Tal went out and found them all by himself? Remember that?

Instead, there was nothing to remember except that he'd broken the rules and then run away like a coward. Nobody would ever know that story though, because he wouldn't tell it. He couldn't tell it. Having to admit to himself that he'd been unable to handle the woods alone was hard enough. No way he was going to admit it to anybody else. And he would just as soon not think about the Christmas present he'd been so sure he wanted. What was he going to do if Daddy gave it to him?

He made a fist and hit the gate, which swung on its hinges. He propped it open and left the yard. The way things were going, he wouldn't have been surprised to find Mama waiting for him in the kitchen, angry and worried. But the house was as quiet as the woods. The oven clock had advanced less than half an hour. Tal's first trip into the night woods had been as brief as it was disastrous. All he'd accomplished was to break his lantern and find out something he didn't like about himself. One scary sound—probably nothing more than a limb falling—had completely defeated him. He was stunned and ashamed. He was also tired and cold. It had been a while since he'd made a good decision. Trying to stay awake in the kitchen would be another bad one. It wasn't going to happen.

Before he went to bed, he checked his face in the bathroom mirror. He looked like he'd been in a fight, which in a way he had. And he'd lost. The place where the limb had caught his face was bruised and swollen. It stung when he washed it. He wondered if he was going to wake up with a black eye. How would he explain that?

He stared at himself in the mirror. The wound that showed was minor compared to the one that didn't. He couldn't wash that one. He couldn't do anything with it. All he could do was go to his room, crawl under his covers, and try not to think about the fact that on top of everything else he still had no idea where his dogs were.

10

Tal's eye was indeed black the next morning. Actually, it was purple. It was also swollen nearly shut, the lower lid having puffed up like a bubble during the night. He tried to cover it with a smear of calamine lotion, but that just made it look worse. He was going to have to hide it. Otherwise, everybody would expect an explanation, and the only one he had was the truth. All he had to do to hide that was keep it to himself. Hiding the injured eye was another matter. He wished that he'd thought to ice it before he went to bed.

The disguise he finally settled on was the pirate patch he'd worn to the Halloween Carnival at school back in October, a lens-shaped piece of black cloth glued to cardboard and attached to an elastic band of the same color. He knew he would have to answer for it, but that would be easier than telling why he had a black eye. The patch did what he wanted it to do. The injury was concealed.

After dressing he stood at his bedroom window and lifted the patch to survey the backyard. Another gray day. The snow had stopped, but enough of it had fallen after he returned from the woods to fill in his footprints. The roofs of the doghouse and the toolshed had thick piles on them. All of the trees were shrouded. It was a beautiful, unreal scene. Something about that much snow seemed fake to Tal. It looked like a painting.

He stared at the open gate of the pen and knew the dogs hadn't come home. He would have seen them by now. They would have been out and about, wondering when the boy who fed them was going to show up. The only positive thought he could get to right then was that at least nobody else was aware of what he'd done. That helped a little but not much. He felt like he might as well have been wearing a sign that had the word CHICKEN written on it in big block letters.

Tal surveyed the scene before him a final time, pulled

the patch back into place, and walked through the house to the kitchen. Papa was at the table having a cup of coffee with Mama.

"Well, if it ain't old Rip Van Winkle," Papa said. "Or is it Long John Silver?"

"It's just me," Tal said. "How's it going, Papa?"

Not too good, he thought. Papa's face was pale, and his skin looked thin and papery. His eyes were bloodshot and seemed too large for his head.

"Oh, I'm able to sit up and take a little nourishment," Papa said. "I ain't officially allowed coffee, but it's Christmas Eve according to my calendar, so I'm having a sip anyway. You dance now, you pay the fiddler later. I'm counting on a fair trade."

"Something the matter with your eye, son?" Mama said.

Tal weighed his situation. He could lie by saying no or he could lie by saying yes. He could even remove the patch and tell the truth. No matter what he did, he would end up feeling bad about it. But he didn't think he could feel much worse than he already did unless he told the truth. So he eliminated that option and decided to lie by saying yes.

"I got something in it," he said.

"Did you get it out?" Mama said.

"I think so," Tal said. "But it's sore. I'm giving it a rest."

"Should I look at it?" Mama said.

Tal shook his head. Mama fixed her eyes on his uncovered one. He had to meet her gaze or she would know he was lying. He wondered if she suspected him and thought maybe she did. He was either going to have to look away and give himself up or change the subject. It reminded him of when he cussed in front of Daddy. The difference was that he felt like he had some control over what would happen this time.

"How're the roads, Papa?" he said.

He kept his eye on Mama's for a beat after he spoke, then he turned his head.

"Near about slick as a candidate for public office is how they are this morning," Papa said. "Truck slipped and slid on me a time or two, but I managed to keep her between the ditches. I was just telling your mama here that I took me a foot ruler to the snow first thing. Picnic table behind the house had eight inches, benches six. That'll average you a stack of seven if I'm ciphering right."

Tal smiled. Papa might not have looked too good, but he was in his usual form when it came to talking.

"I expected you to be in here when I got up," Mama said.

"I kept nodding off," Tal said. "They weren't coming, and I got tired of trying to stay awake so I just went on to bed."

"Took the watched-pot-never-boils approach, did you?" Papa said. "Heard about your dogs, Tal, and I'm ready to form a search party when you are. It's why I came on out."

"Thanks, Papa," Tal said. "Y'all heard from Daddy yet?"

He hadn't intended this question to be what got him off the hook regarding the patch and his injured eye, but when he saw the glances Mama and Papa exchanged and heard Papa clear his throat he knew that he was out of that trouble for the time being. He also knew the answer to his question.

"He called," Mama said. "It's an icy mess down there."

Tal waited for her to continue, but she was finished.

"So he's not coming then," he said.

"He can't, honey," Mama said. "Him and some of the offshore guys're getting rooms in Morgan City until they think it's safe to drive. It may be tomorrow, but he said it's just wait and see for right now."

Tal leaned against the counter and crossed his arms. He stared at the floor. Everything seemed wrong to him, and he was about to say so when Jessie came in from playing outside. She had on a hooded coat and a muffler, and she was tracking snow. The little bit of her face that wasn't hidden was as red as an apple.

"Cold enough for you out there this morning, young lady?" Papa said.

Jessie hugged herself and shook her shoulders to indicate how cold she was. Mama and Papa laughed, but Tal was too preoccupied to be amused. Daddy was stuck in South Louisiana, Papa looked old and sick, the dogs were lost, and he was a coward and a liar. He wished he'd stayed in bed and was dreaming all of this.

"Snowmen, Talmidge," Jessie said. "Remember? Hey, why you got that eye thing on for? This is Christmas, not Halloween."

"I'm early," Tal said.

"You're making a mess, Jessie," Mama said. "You need to either come in and take those boots off or go on back out."

"Don't be long, Talmidge," Jessie said. "You promised."

"In a minute," Tal said.

He waited for her to leave.

"Daddy's not even going to try today?" he said.

"No reason to," Papa said. "They're socked plumb in down there. Storm broke every record in the file."

Tal couldn't stand it. Tears filled his eyes, making the injured one sting. He knew he wouldn't be able to control his voice, so he just nodded. Mama rose from her chair and put a hand on his shoulder. He didn't mind if she saw him, but he didn't want Papa to know that he was crying.

"It's okay, sweetie," Mama said.

"No," Tal said. "There's nothing okay about anything. Everything's wrong."

He jerked away from Mama's hand and moved to the sink, where he stood with his head down.

"Whoa now," Papa said. "It ain't as bad as all that, Talmidge. You got to look on the bright side."

Tal turned. He was mad at Papa for trying to make him feel better, and he was mad at himself for not being able to do it. He was mad at everything and everybody.

"What bright side?" he said. "You show me one and I'll look on it. But you can't because there ain't one to show."

Papa raised his eyebrows, then he began to turn his coffee mug with his fingers. Tal's angry words had hurt him. That was as plain as the snow on the ground. All he'd done was drive out on a bad road to lend a hand when he probably didn't feel like it and now this.

"I think you need to quit feeling sorry for yourself, son," Mama said.

She walked to the pantry and got her mop. Tal watched her swab the puddle of melted snow Jessie had left. He knew he should apologize to Papa, but he was too mad at Mama for being right about feeling sorry for himself to do anything except give all the way in to just that.

"This ain't Christmas," he said. "I hate it."

The best thing that happened to him that morning was that Mama and Papa did not try to stop him when he left the kitchen. He expected one of them to as he put on his coat. Neither said a word.

Outside, Jessie had her snow family all planned.

"I want six," she said.

"You said four last night," Tal said.

"There needs to be Mimi and Papa ones, too," Jessie said. "I forgot to think about them."

Tal sighed. If he hadn't already treated everybody unfairly enough for one day he might have told Jessie to build her own snow family. But he didn't have the energy to deal with upsetting her. There was a chance that Mama and Papa would understand why he'd acted the way he had. Jessie would have no idea.

"Let's make six then," he said.

"Six!" Jessie said.

Tal hadn't expected to get much help from her and he didn't. He did all of the work while she did all of the bossing around, which suited him just fine. It gave him a chance to think. He didn't even threaten to quit when she lost interest in the job and started complaining about the cold. His mind was on what he was going to say to Papa.

"I'm freezing, Talmidge," Jessie said.

"Well, go on in," Tal said. "It's no use you freezing."

"Will you still finish them if I do?"

"Sure. Why wouldn't I?"

"Because. Are you and Papa going looking for the dogs later?"

"I think so."

"I miss Claudia. LC and Pete, too, but mostly her. She's so little."

"Yeah, but she's tough."

"You look funny with that deal on."

Tal considered telling her why he was wearing the patch but didn't because he wasn't sure he could trust her to keep a secret that important, if it even was a secret. Mama was no fool. She just hadn't pressed him very hard.

"Didn't you say you were cold?" he said.

"It's like my toes are asleep, they're so froze."

"Get Mama to make you a fire."

"Papa makes bigger ones."

"Then get him to."

"I'm coming back out with clothes for the snow family when I get warm," Jessie said. "And hats."

He watched her skip toward the house. He was amazed that she hadn't mentioned Daddy, but maybe she didn't know. If she did, it didn't seem to bother her. It bothered him, though. Knowing that Daddy definitely wouldn't be home for Christmas Eve and might not for Christmas Day bothered him a lot. There was something unreal about it, too. There was something unreal about everything that morning.

The snow wasn't any easier to pack than it had been the night before. Tal did the best he could with it. After a while he wasn't thinking about anything but the work. His mind was as numb as his hands.

He was rolling the head for the next-to-last figure when he heard footsteps. He didn't have to look to know that it was Papa crunching through the snow. He played like he hadn't noticed and kept working. Papa stopped to strike a match. A moment later Tal breathed in the fragrance of burning pipe tobacco. It was tough and good. It was Papa. Tal lifted the head and set it into place.

"I didn't really mean that about Christmas," he said.

"Sure you did," Papa said. "Whenever a fellow says he didn't mean something it's always a sign he couldn't have been more sincere at the time. He spoke his mind is what he done."

Tal turned. Papa walked over and stood between two of the snowmen.

"Pure honesty's a funny thing, Tal," he said. "What you're telling me now ain't that you didn't mean it, because you did. You just wish you'd kept it to yourself. There's things to think and say, then there's things to just think. Good luck seeing the difference in time to stay out of trouble."

"You mad?" Tal said.

"Why, hair no," Papa said.

"I thought you'd be ready to bust me one."

"There was a time I might've been."

"I'm sorry, Papa."

"Tell your mama that, if you're worried about some-body being mad. I believe I got her defused for you, but a little sweet talk wouldn't hurt your cause none."

"Probably not."

Papa looked at Tal's work and frowned.

"What in the world are these heaps suppose to be," he said. "Modern art?"

"They're Jessie's snow family," Tal said. "Five down, one to go."

"Well, let's get in gear. I'm about ready to take a spin and see if we can't scare them hounds of yours out from the piney woods."

They made the final figure together. Tal noticed Papa's breathing as they worked. He was doing it through his mouth, and it sounded bad to Tal.

"You all right?" he said.

Papa nodded, but Tal feared that he was in worse shape than he was letting on.

11

Papa's plan was to work as many of the two-tracks and dirt roads as they could and see what turned up in the way of lost dogs.

"I'll try not to get us stuck," he said as he eased his pickup onto Thousand Pines Road.

Getting stuck was one thing Tal knew he didn't need to worry about. Being a retired rural mail carrier, Papa could get where he was going. He could also get back. He'd spent a lifetime doing it. Tal just hoped they had three more passengers with them when they returned to the house.

"Find us some radio," Papa said. "We'll go with my usual brand if it's all the same to you."

"Why you like country music so much?" Tal said.

"Same reason you will when you grow into it," Papa said. "Because it's about things that matter."

Tal set the dial on the local station. It was nothing but solid country from sign-on to sign-off, seven days a week. The only exceptions were a church service every Sunday and, during the season, Oil Camp High football games— live on Friday night, taped on Saturday morning. Tal usually listened to the replays even of games he'd been to. Like most of his friends, he planned to be a Roughneck himself when he got old enough.

Papa turned the radio up. The song that was playing was slow and mournful.

"They'd teach Hank in school as required material if I was in charge," Papa said.

"Who's Hank?" Tal said.

"That's Hank," Papa said. "Hank Williams. Listen to him. He's a flat-out poet. Was anyway. He's gone now."

Tal listened for a moment.

"Sure does sound sad," he said.

"Hank'll sound every way a fellow can," Papa said. "Sometimes sad, sometimes desperate, sometimes even happy or silly. But he's always true, always right. Too bad he drank hisself to death so young."

"How old was he?" Tal said.

"Twenty-nine," Papa said. "That might seem old to you, but it ain't. Not by quite a while. Just let's listen."

In this particular song, Hank kept saying that he was so lonesome he could cry. Tal identified with the feeling. Now that he'd made up with Papa he wasn't as down as he had been, but he was still having a tough time seeing the bright side. The things that were bothering him were bigger and more threatening than usual. These weren't the kind that would just work themselves out. His life seemed to have taken a turn in the wrong direction, falling apart like the weather had the day before, from clear and mild to cloudy and cold. Nothing made sense anymore.

He glanced at Papa, who was seventy-three. After so many years of living, he must have had the world pretty much figured out. No matter what happened, he probably wasn't too surprised because he'd seen it before.

"I need to ask you something, Papa," Tal said.

The Hank song ended and was replaced by a commercial for Piggly Wiggly. Papa turned the radio off.

"Fire when ready," he said.

"Remember a while ago you telling me I got to look on the bright side?" Tal said:

"What I remember is you didn't think much of it at the time," Papa said.

"No, but I'm wondering. Do you do that?"

"Do I look on the bright side?"

"Uh-huh."

"I suppose so. Try to anyway."

"What if you can't see it?"

"Then you keep looking."

"Does it get easier or harder?"

Papa tapped the brakes and steered the truck left, off of Thousand Pines and onto a snow-covered dirt road. He looked from side to side as he drove. Tal thought he must either not have heard the question or had no ready answer for it.

"There's a two-track off this somewhere along in here," Papa said. "Yonder it is."

He pointed to an opening, pulled up to it, and stopped the truck. He showed Tal his pipe. It had a curved stem and a bowl shaped like an acorn.

"You mind?" Papa said.

Tal recalled how ragged Papa's breathing had been when they finished the last snowman.

"Go ahead," he said.

"Much obliged," Papa said.

The truck engine was still running. Papa cracked his window and lit up. He smoked for a moment, thinking. Tal waited. It was hard for him to reconcile the way the tobacco smelled with how dangerous it was.

"I suppose that whether it gets easier or harder's primarily a matter of how a fellow's made, Talmidge," Papa said.

He shifted in his seat so that he was looking at Tal.

"How do you know how you're made?" Tal said.

"Oh, you get presented with one thing and another," Papa said. "They'll show you if you pay any attention. It ain't so much what happens as how you respond to it."

"It must be going to get harder for me then," Tal said.

"Don't you reckon it's a mite early in the day for you to be making that call?" Papa said.

"What do you mean?"

"Well, last time I added up the candles on a birthday cake of yours there wasn't but I believe ten—not counting the one to grow on. You ain't hardly started yet."

"Yeah, but I'm not doing too good with my responses lately."

"Nobody's holding this morning against you, Talmidge," Papa said. "A fellow's got every right to get up on the wrong side of his bed now and again. Shoot, I'd been out of sorts too if my dogs was lost and my daddy was about to miss Christmas."

"It ain't just that," he said.

Papa remained silent. The windows were getting fogged over. Tal stared at the gray-and-white blur the world had become.

"If I tell you what else it is, would you keep it a secret for me, Papa?" he said.

"You say to and I wouldn't breathe a word if it'd save my life."

Tal turned so that he was again facing Papa.

"I came out here by myself last night," he said.

"I see," Papa said.

"No, you don't," Tal said. "Mama told me not to and you know what Daddy says. But I thought I could find the dogs."

"Would've thought the same thing," Papa said.

Tal realized that Papa did see. He could tell him anything, even the truth.

"I got scared, Papa," he said. "I didn't even look for them much. I went a little away from the house, then I heard something and ran. My lantern's out there somewhere, busted all to pieces because I fell down and dropped it."

Papa's pipe had gone out. He drew on it a couple of times and removed it from his mouth. His breathing was fast and shallow.

"Let me tell you a secret of my own, Talmidge," he said. "I'm a right smart piece down the road and I've seen a thing or two along the way. Some good, some not, some hard to tell which. One lesson I've learned is that you never know what's around the next bend. This past year I come face to face with one of those things you'd just as soon not have to if you had your druthers. I know the road can't go on forever, but such a direct reminder as I got when my heart attacked me put a real fear into my bones."

"What're you scared of?" Tal said.

"Same thing you are, son," Papa said. "The son-of-a-bitching dark."

Neither of them said anything for a while, then Papa suddenly reached across and horsed Tal's leg.

"Speaking of which, did a tree happen to jump out in front of you last night, Talmidge?"

Tal hesitated a beat, but he knew Papa wouldn't have said that if he didn't consider it part of their secret.

"A limb sort of did," Tal said.

"Mind showing me the result?" Papa said.

Tal lifted the patch. Papa whistled through his teeth.

"You must've been sore afraid like the abiding shepherds," he said. "Scared the fool out of them old boys when that angel dropped in to let them know what happened in Bethlehem that night."

Papa began to laugh. At first it was just a chuckle. Then it changed into a full-fledged guffaw that was contagious. The two of them would laugh for a while and stop, get tickled all over again, and laugh some more. Eventually, Papa was coughing as much as he was laughing. His face was flushed and he made a dry, screeching sound that alarmed Tal.

"Papa?" he said.

Still coughing like his lungs were disintegrating, Papa held up a hand to indicate that he was okay. Tal waited. The fit was the worst he'd heard Papa have. It was like listening to somebody choking. Finally it passed. Papa drew a couple of deep, wheezing breaths.

"Hoo, lord," he said.

He wiped his eyes with his thumb.

"Wish I'd seen it," he said. "Must've been some kind of a run. You just outsmarted yourself is all, which when you're in the woods at night by your lonesome is about as unique as having a belly button. Happens to everybody. But you can get sore afraid anywhere, Talmidge. The trick is to ignore it, tell whatever it is you think's scaring you to go to hell. Else, you'll be slamming into a tree every time you turn around. Make sense?"

"Pretty much," Tal said. "Is it like why you keep on smoking your pipe when everybody tells you not to?"

"Never thought of it that way," Papa said. "Could be, I reckon. Could be. Not that I breathe it down, understand. I just savor the taste."

Tal was learning that the only person you ever really lie to is yourself.

They spent the heart of the afternoon driving from one place to the next, parking, and getting out of the truck. They'd whistle and listen, then they'd call and listen. Their breath trailed away from their mouths like shreds of cloth. Every time they stopped Tal walked among the flocked trees expecting at least one of the beagles to come running toward him. He saw several rabbits and squirrels, quite a few birds, two bucks and, amazingly, a fox. The dogs never showed.

Papa didn't turn the radio on as they drove slowly back to the house. The heater was blowing full blast, but Tal couldn't get warm. He just sat shivering. Like the day, his hope was fading. He was beginning to wonder if LC, Pete, and Claudia were gone for good.

12

As promised, Jessie had dressed her snow family. Sporting bill caps and scarves, the six figures stood in the front yard like visitors from another world who couldn't quite make up their minds about how to deal with this one. Tal thought he would fit right in with them.

"Looks like our Jessie's been on the job," Papa said.

He stopped the truck to let Tal out.

"Thanks for looking with me, Papa," Tal said.

"Enjoyed the time," Papa said. "Don't give plumb up, Talmidge."

"I'm trying not to," Tal said.

"That's right," Papa said. "Miracles have happened around this time of year, you know—not that I mean to say we're all the way to needing one yet. You just hang in there."

"Okay," Tal said. "See you this evening, Papa."

"Looking forward to it," Papa said.

Tal watched Papa drive away before he walked around to the back of the house. He was stamping snow off of his boots when Jessie opened the door and almost knocked him over with the screen.

"Dang, Jessie," he said.

"You got to come see, Talmidge," Jessie said. "And be quiet. You won't believe."

"Won't believe what?" Tal said.

"Just hurry," Jessie said.

Inside, Tal slipped his gloves and boots off but left on his coat. The house was warm. It smelled like Mama was busy in the kitchen. Jessie grabbed Tal's hand. She led him into the front room, which was dark except for a low fire and the Christmas tree lights. The ones on the mantel were off.

"What's the deal?" Tal said.

"Shh," Jessie said. "Look."

When Tal's uncovered eye adjusted to the gloom he spotted LC and Pete curled up on the rug in front of the fireplace. They were sound asleep. He glanced around for Claudia but didn't see her. For a moment it was like everything inside of him had turned to ice. But the sensation was brief, gone almost as soon as it came upon him. LC and Pete were home!

He wanted to rush over and throw himself down beside the dogs. He wanted to rub their ears and feel their tongues on his face. He wanted to squeeze them until they struggled to get away. But they looked so peaceful that he fought off the urge to disturb them. Instead, he picked Jessie up by the waist.

"Talmidge!" Jessie said.

He set her down. LC and Pete both stirred but didn't wake up. LC moaned. One of Pete's rear legs twitched.

"I never saw them so asleep," Tal said. "They're wore all the way out."

"They're full all the way up, too," Jessie said. "Mama let them straight in when they got here. You'll never guess what happened then."

"That you, Tal?"

Mama appeared in the archway between the kitchen and the front room. She was drying her hands with a dish towel.

Tal moved quickly to her and hugged her with all of his strength, something he hadn't done in a while. Usually his hugs were one-armed and brief.

"I'll accept this as your apology for being a horse's rear end this morning," she said.

"That's what it is," Tal said. "I'm sorry, Mama."

"You ought to be," Mama said. "I take it you mended your fences with Papa?"

"I did," Tal said.

"Mama said she was mad as blue blazes at you, Talmidge," Jessie said. "That's really mad."

"What happened after the dogs came in?" he said.

"Lots," Jessie said. "Tell him, Mama."

"Come in here to the scene of the crime and I will," Mama said.

The warm, steamy smell of the kitchen made Tal's mouth water. He hadn't eaten all day long, and he was so hungry that his head ached. He lifted the lid of the largest pot on the stove and spooned up a bite.

"Mmmm-mmm," he said. "Except wait a minute. There's no meat in here."

"That's because it's inside of LC and Pete," Jessie said. "They gobbled it all up. Mama let them."

"No way," Tal said.

"She did," Jessie said. "The dogs ate the chicken vittles right off the floor. You should've seen them, Talmidge."

"I wouldn't have believed it," Tal said.

"I still almost can't hardly believe it myself," Mama said. "I was getting ready to bone a chicken for that gumbo. I had it cooling in the sink and was looking out the window. I wasn't thinking about the dogs as much as about you sitting there waiting for them last night, Tal. Then, just all of I mean a sudden, there they were. LC and Pete. They strolled in the yard like it was any old day."

"That's when she dropped the chicken," Jessie said. "It was a big one, and it went all over the place because where Mama dropped it wasn't the sink. It was the floor."

"Which I couldn't tell you how," Mama said. "I must've just picked it up and turned and flung it down when I saw them. I have no idea. I was so relieved that I ran to the door and called to them before they even passed the pen. Well, that was a mistake because they came zooming in here like a couple of hurricanes."

"And chicken was everywhere," Jessie said. "Me and Mama tried to shoo LC and Pete, but they wouldn't shoo. They was too busy eating."

"How did y'all keep them from fighting over it?" Tal said.

"It was boiled so soft that it plopped and splattered every whichaway," Mama said. "I knew it was a lost cause, so I just took a broom and scooted a little here and a little there. The dogs were too caught up in staying with their own pile to even notice each other."

"They ate and ate," Jessie said. "Juice and meat and bones—all gone."

"So we're having ourselves veggie gumbo this Christmas Eve," Mama said. "What do you think?"

Tal sampled another bite and nodded.

"Are LC and Pete inside dogs now?" he said.

"Hardly," Mama said. "I just didn't have the heart to put them back out when I saw them so comfortable by the fire."

"I wish I knew Claudia's somewhere that warm," Tal said.

"It'd be nice to think," Mama said.

The back and forth emotions of the day and the fact that he hadn't slept well the night before combined at that moment to make Tal as weary as he could ever remember being. Still wearing his coat, he trudged into the front room and lay down beside LC and Pete. Their breathing was deep and steady. A few minutes later Tal's was, too.

13

Tal slept so soundly that if he dreamed he had no memory of it when he awakened. LC and Pete were sitting on either side of him, their tails thumping against the rug. He put an arm around the dogs and drew them near.

"Don't y'all ever do that again," he said.

He heard voices in the kitchen. He must have slept for quite a while because Mimi and Papa had arrived and were talking with Mama and Jessie. Tal held LC and Pete the way he'd wanted to earlier. They were strong and sturdy. They had a secret he would never know. He hugged them hard. They stayed beside him when he let them go.

He sat up and took off his patch. He opened his injured

eye wide a couple of times. He touched it and winced, wondering how it looked. Probably not good enough to show anybody, he thought. He replaced the patch and stood. He needed a shower because he had slept in his coat and was sweating. He started for the kitchen. LC and Pete trotted ahead of him.

"What's the hurry?" he said. "I heard y'all done ate the chicken."

He recalled the scene Mama and Jessie had described. He wasn't sure which part he liked better, the dogs eating the dropped chicken or Mama letting them inside. She'd never done that. It was a good story. It would have been perfect with Claudia in it. Tal thought about her. He pictured her in his mind. He wondered if he would ever see her again.

In the kitchen, Jessie was sitting on the counter beside the sink. She kicked her heels against the cabinet door below. Mama and Papa were standing by the stove. Mimi was perched on the stool Tal had used the night before. Everybody was dressed up. Papa had on a tie. His face was freshly shaved but still pale. His little bit of hair was slicked straight back.

"LC and Pete're hunting for another chicken, y'all," Jessie said.

"They'll be doing that every time they come in here from now on," Papa said. "It's psychology. Dog, human, don't matter. You always look where something was at next time you're there."

"Well, they better look good because this is the last time they'll be looking in here," Mama said.

"You plan to say hidy to me, Talmidge?" Mimi said.

"Hey, Mimi," Tal said. "I'd hug you, but I probably smell like a polecat I been sweating so much. I like that dress."

"Why, thank you, honey," Mimi said. "I sewed it myself. I like your eye patch. Is it for a reason or just fun?"

"I got something in it," Tal said.

"I hope it's okay," Mimi said.

Tal glanced at Papa, who lifted an eyebrow.

"He won't let me look at it," Mama said.

"What's a polecat?" Jessie said.

"A skunk," Tal said.

"Maybe you ought to get out of that coat and set with us a spell, Talmidge," Papa said. "On second thought, if you smell like a polecat maybe you better keep it on."

"You hush, Papa," Mimi said. "Bring yourself over here

right now, Talmidge Cotton. I'd hug my grandson if he smelled like ten polecats."

Tal gave Mimi a hug.

"You smell like all boy to me," she said.

"Which ain't necessarily a compliment," Papa said.

"Oh, yes it is," Mimi said. "I made your favorite, Talmidge."

"Carrot cake," Tal said.

"With extra pecans," Mimi said.

"Go on and wash up if you're going to, Tal," Mama said. "Supper's in half an hour."

Jessie had jumped down from the counter and was on the floor stroking LC and Pete.

"You want me to put them on out?" Tal said.

Mama gave each of the dogs a quick pat on the head.

"I almost feel bad," she said. "But I don't want them getting ideas about being inside."

"Mimi and Papa're spending the night because of the snow on the road, Talmidge," Jessie said.

"Y'all are?" Tal said.

"We'd just have to turn around and come back out here in the morning," Mimi said. "You don't mind, do you?"

"Who'd mind that?" Tal said.

"I just hope Santa Claus knows where to park my Cadillac," Papa said. "That's what I asked him for again, as usual. Maybe he'll have a change of heart this year and take me off the Naughty side of his list."

"Santa Claus knows where everybody's suppose to be, Papa," Jessie said.

They all laughed, including Tal. Papa coughed.

"I'll get the dogs for you, Tal," he said.

"Don't you go out there and light up that blasted pipe," Mimi said. "I'll be watching."

"You and Santa Claus," Papa said. "Come on, LC. Here, Pete. Let's go."

"Smoking's bad for you, Papa," Jessie said. "It turns your insides black. The nurse at school showed us gross pictures."

"You tell him all about those pictures, sweetheart," Mimi said. "He won't listen to the rest of us. Maybe he will to you."

"I feel a case of hard of hearing coming on," Papa said.

He clicked his tongue so the dogs would follow him outside.

"Stubborn old fool," Mimi said. "He had a coughing fit

before we left for out here I thought was going to be the end of him right then and there. When he finished I told him to ask me what I want for Christmas and he said he knew what I was fixing to say."

"Which was what?" Tal said.

"For him to put that pipe in a drawer and leave it," Mimi said.

"Did you say it?" Jessie said.

"I most certainly did," Mimi said.

"Good for you," Mama said. "What did he say back?"

"He said he'd think on it," Mimi said.

"Well, maybe he will," Tal said.

"Maybe so," Mimi said. "I just wish he'd be reasonable. He claims not to inhale, but who's he fooling except an old man? I swear. Sometimes I think the principal reason he carries that thing is to get my goat."

Tal knew that Papa didn't use his pipe to get Mimi's goat. He had other reasons, ones that were his alone. They didn't have anything to do with anybody else. Papa's pipe was a complicated and confusing thing. Tal understood it, but he knew he would have had no luck trying to put it into words. It would be like trying to say why the dog who wasn't there was the one he most wanted to see. How could he do that and still let them know that the ones who were there meant everything to him too? How could he explain how he felt about anything without being misunderstood? He couldn't. He just felt it, that's all, and Papa just smoked his pipe.

Something was happening to Tal. The world had thrown so much at him during the past couple of days that he didn't know what to think anymore. He wished he could empty his mind altogether. Maybe then things would start making sense again.

14

Tal's family had eaten Christmas Eve supper with Mimi and Papa since before he had a memory of it. They alternated houses every year. If the meal was at Tal's, Mama was responsible for the main courses and Mimi brought the desserts. If it was at Mimi and Papa's, the cooking duties were switched. Regardless of where they were, once everybody was seated Daddy always opened the Bible and read the first sixteen verses of the second chapter of Luke. Then Papa would bless the food. This year, Tal was going to read in Daddy's absence.

His hair was still damp from the shower when he sat down at the table, which was covered with a white cloth and set with Mama's best dishes and silverware. The silver rested on her special-occasion napkins, also cloth. All of the food had been transferred from the pots and pans it was cooked in to serving bowls and platters. Mama had fixed enough to provide several days' worth of leftovers, as was her holiday custom. In addition to the meatless gumbo, cornbread, and rolls the size of softballs, there were pork chops to go with three kinds of beans—butter, string, and baby lima—carrots, macaroni and cheese, a rice and broccoli casserole, plain rice for the gumbo, candied yams, fruit salad, and ice tea. On the counter were Mimi's carrot cake, a Karo pecan pie, and pyramids of brownies, pralines, and white divinity.

"Have mercy," Papa said. "You could feed Communist China with this. Think we can put a respectable dent in it, Tal? Here, let me work on that noose for you."

Daddy had taught Tal to tie a tie, but he still needed help getting the knot straight.

"There you go," Papa said.

"My, doesn't everyone look nice," Mimi said. "It's all beautiful, Beth. Just beautiful."

"I wish we could dress up and eat these kind of vittles every night," Jessie said. "It's like being kings and queens."

"Except for one minor detail," Mama said. "No servants."

The only light in the room came from six slender candles, three on the table and three on the counter among Mimi's sweets. Tal looked around. It was almost worth being half strangled by a tie for. The only thing wrong with it was Daddy's empty chair.

Mama handed him the Bible, already opened to the page.

Tal knew Luke's words as well as he knew the alphabet, but he decided not to try to recite the verses from memory. Taking Daddy's place was too important to chance making a mistake. He drew a breath and began to read: " 'And it came to pass in those days, that there went out a decree from Caesar Augustus, that all the world should be taxed . . .' "

Making out the tiny print with one eye in the flickering light wasn't easy. Tal leaned toward the book. That helped. He got through seven verses without any trouble. Then he reached the eighth, where the abiding shepherds were waiting. Remembering what happened after Papa asked him if he'd been sore afraid like them that afternoon, he had to fight off getting tickled. The remaining passages were mined with words like "lo" and "tidings" and, worst of all, "swaddling clothes." Under normal circumstances, none of them would have bothered him. They were serious Bible words. Now they all struck him as hysterically funny and he thought he was going to suffocate trying not to ruin everything by laughing. Somehow he managed to overcome the urge and delivered the shepherds safely to Bethlehem. There they found the baby Jesus. He finished in a breathless rush and sat back in his chair. It seemed like he'd been reading for an hour.

"Boy, you sure can read fast, Talmidge," Jessie said.

"It does say that they came with haste," Papa said. "I believe they made record time this evening."

"You did just fine, hon," Mimi said. "Those are wonderful verses, fast or slow."

"Papa?" Mama said.

"Y'all bow your heads with me," Papa said.

In his blessing he was asking that Daddy be allowed a safe trip from Morgan City as soon as possible when Jessie interrupted him to whisper, "Say Claudia, too, from wherever she's at." Papa added the request, after which the five of them joined hands to recite the Lord's Prayer.

"Let's see now," Mama said. "I guess everybody just start your plates around and put some of whatever's in front of you on each one when it comes. Jessie, you can serve us all a yam."

"Why do some people say to forgive them their debts and some people their trespasses?" Jessie said.

"Start them which way, Mama?" Tal said.

"Clockwise," Mama said.

" 'Debts' is Baptist, I believe," Papa said. "Straight from the book."

"Send your bowl, too, if you want to see what gumbo is like without meat," Mama said. "Talmidge, that rice is right there. You do it up and I'll ladle over it. Remember, this is an experiment, y'all, thanks to my little helpers this afternoon."

" 'As we forgive those who trespass against us' sounds so much more poetic to my ear than 'as we forgive our debtors' does," Mimi said.

"That's because it is," Papa said. "They ain't interested in poetry over to the First Baptist. They leave that to us Methodists."

"What does it even mean?" Jessie said.

"It's when you go somewhere you ain't suppose to," Tal said. "Y'all say if you want more of this rice than I'm giving."

"It's also when you do something you shouldn't," Mama said.

Tal realized that both definitions described what he'd done the night before. He glanced at Mama but she was busy putting a serving of the casserole on Mimi's plate.

"Just half a dab of that," Mimi said.

"Watching your figure?" Papa said.

"Somebody has to," Mimi said.

"Somebody's been doing it for fifty years," Papa said. "And he likes what he sees a little more every day. Could be that there's a little more to like."

"Honestly," Mimi said.

"What's 'debts'?" Jessie said.

"You sure do ask a lot of questions, Jessie," Tal said.

"It's how to learn," Jessie said. "Mrs. Smiley at school told us there's no such thing as a stupid one either."

"And she's right," Mama said.

" 'Debts' is when you owe somebody something," Papa said.

"Like an apology," Mimi said.

She gave Papa a look.

"It was a compliment," Papa said.

"Could've fooled me," Mimi said. "What if I went on a starvation diet and got skinny as a pencil?"

"Then I'd adjust," Papa said. "I've heard tell that less can be more, depending on a fellow's perspective."

"Could you mean to forgive your money debts?" Jessie said. "That's funny to pray about."

"Not if you have some," Papa said.

"Law, would you look at this plate," Mimi said.

"So much for that diet," Papa said.

"Thanks for doing pork chops, Mama," Tal said.

"They're just for you," Mama said.

"But you have to share," Papa said.

"Be careful now, Papa," Mimi said. "You know what the doctor says about you eating fried."

"Surely nobody's ever died of a pork chop," Papa said.

"I wouldn't mind it," Tal said.

Each of them now had a full plate, and they settled in to eat. They did it until they were stuffed, then they did it some more. At one point or another everything on the table was praised by somebody as the best of its kind that had ever been served. Tal said he would put Mama's chops up against anybody's. To prove it he had three.

"Better let me try another round of them beans, Beth," Papa said. "And I'll take a second yam there, too, Jessie, if you wouldn't mind. Surely the doctor won't object. I think I can reach the bread."

"Don't the rest of y'all get shy on me now," Mama said. "There's still plenty of everything."

"I'm about ready for a piece of carrot cake myself," Tal said. "I got just enough room."

"I couldn't eat another bite," Mimi said. "Oh, maybe a praline."

"My belly's pooched out like a ball," Jessie said.

One by one, they all reached the point of wanting no more.

"Mighty good," Papa said. "Mighty fine."

"Me and Talmidge get our one present next," Jessie said.

"After we clear the table," Mama said.

"We could leave it," Jessie said.

"We could," Mama said. "But let's don't."

Tal and Papa took care of the dishes, Papa washing while Tal dried and stacked. Mama and Mimi secured the leftovers for the refrigerator and made a bowl of scraps for the dogs. Jessie carried the tablecloth and the napkins to the laundry room on her way to decide which present she was going to open.

Unlike some of their friends, who opened all of their wrapped presents on Christmas Eve, Tal and Jessie were only allowed one apiece. Tal normally spent hours debating his choice. He hadn't done much of that this year because the only thing he wanted couldn't be wrapped. Now that he'd had a taste of being in the woods alone, his desire for that one seemed like something from another life.

"I know what I'd give you if I could," Papa said.

Tal was rinsing his last glass. He nodded. He didn't have to ask what Papa meant.

Jessie changed her mind several times before finally selecting the oblong package from Mimi and Papa that she'd originally said she would. It was just what she'd predicted, a Barbie dressed as an LSU cheerleader.

"There's a right comely figure for you, Papa," Mimi said. "Are you awake over there?"

"Enough to hear you," Papa said. "Miss Barbie keeps herself a shade too trim for my taste."

Jessie thanked Mimi and Papa by giving them hugs.

"I hope this one don't get lost in the crowd," Papa said.

"She won't," Jessie said. "All of my Barbies are friends."

After rummaging through his gifts, Tal picked one that he hadn't noticed before. It was wrapped in newspaper, and it was from Papa. Tal expected it to be a football. He was wrong. It was a lantern.

"Last-minute idea," Papa said.

"Thanks, Papa," Tal said.

He hoped the others didn't notice that his face had turned red.

"Could we open two this year?" Jessie said.

"No, ma'am," Mama said.

"I knew it," Jessie said.

"Don't pout," Mama said.

"I'm not," Jessie said. "I was just seeing."

They spent the rest of the evening watching *A Christmas Carol* on television. Mama popped a huge bowl of corn, Papa poked up a fresh blaze in the fireplace, and they gathered around to follow Ebeneezer Scrooge on his famous journey through time with the three ghosts who show him all the mistakes he made in the past, is making in the present, and will make in the future if he doesn't change his ways.

For a while, Tal was absorbed in the movie. Then he

found himself thinking about Claudia again. Her absence was like a wound, a literal thing he could feel. It wasn't like Daddy's. He knew for sure that Daddy would be back eventually. Claudia might not. It was possible that she was as gone as yesterday and that he would never know where she went or what happened to her. It was a terrible thought to have. He shook his head as if to keep himself from falling asleep. He watched Scrooge, who was brushing snow off of his own tombstone. Scrooge was lucky. He had a chance to turn a sad ending into a happy one.

"That's a scary ghost," Jessie said.

"Not really," Tal said. "I wouldn't mind him visiting me tonight."

"I'd hide," Jessie said.

The grownups smiled sleepily. All Tal could do was draw a corner of his mouth back.

15

Jessie was having a time trying to make up her mind what kind of a snack to set out for Santa Claus before she went to bed.

"It's always milk and cookies," she said. "I want to leave something different for a special surprise this year."

"A bowl of your mama's gumbo'd surprise him twice," Papa said.

"How twice?" Jessie said.

"First, that it wasn't milk and a cookie," Papa said. "Second, that it don't have a lick of meat in it."

"Maybe he's a vegetablearian," Jessie said.

"It's vegetarian, Jess," Tal said. "And he ain't."

"You don't know what he is, Talmidge," Jessie said. "Does he, Papa."

It wasn't a question.

"No, but he does have a point," Papa said. "You don't need to look at Santa Claus too very long to figure he's got more than just a little bit of truck driver in him. And if I know my truck drivers I'd say that what the old elf'd really go for by the time he enters Oil Camp airspace is a chicken-fried steak and a cup of strong black coffee."

"We don't have that," Jessie said.

"He's kidding," Tal said.

"I'm not," Jessie said.

Papa rubbed the top of her head.

"I know it, kid," he said. "Whatever you go with'll be just fine, I guarantee. The thought's the thing, and nobody understands that fact better than Saint Nick."

In the end, Jessie put together a plate of Mimi's desserts—brownies, pralines, divinity, and a slice of carrot cake. Instead of milk, she poured a glass of ice water. Then, with great care, she set the treats on the brick ledge in front of the fireplace.

"There," she said. "He can take his pick."

"He's definitely got one," Papa said.

Tal wondered if Jessie had ever had the thought that Santa Claus might not be an actual person. Half of him felt sorry for her. The other half was jealous. He remembered what it was like going to bed on Christmas Eve knowing without a doubt that Santa was on his way to your house. There was nothing more exciting. You could hardly sleep, and if you believed and listened hard enough you'd swear when you got up the next morning that you had heard the big sleigh land during the night. And presents would be under the tree to verify it, unwrapped presents he had brought just for you. Even more convincing was the partially eaten snack you'd left for him. You didn't mind that Santa never finished all of it because you knew everybody else left him a snack, too, and that he was bound to be getting full. The only thing that mattered was that he'd paid you a visit, and you believed in him with all of your heart.

This was the second Christmas Eve that Tal would go to bed knowing that Santa Claus wasn't coming and never had. Having heard rumors at school, he had asked Mama to tell him the truth once and for all.

"Does he really come, or is it just you and Daddy?" he said. "I need to know because they called me a baby for believing in him. I almost got in a fight over it."

"I believe in him," Mama said. "You think they'd call me a baby?"

"No, but do you believe in him because he's real or because of something else?" Tal said.

"I believe in him because that's what makes him real," Mama said.

"So he's not?"

Mama thought about her answer for a long time before she gave it.

"He's not real like you and I are," she said. "But there is a Santa Claus."

"I don't get it," Tal said. "What do you mean?"

"I mean he's a part of what Christmas is," Mama said. "He's an idea. Christmas is an idea. You have to believe in that idea. If you didn't, it'd just be another day."

At first Tal was glad to have the news. He could hardly wait to get to school the next day and tell his friends what he'd learned. Later, after he'd let them know and joined them in laughing at all the babies who did believe, he felt sad in a way he didn't understand.

Once Jessie was tucked in, Tal and Papa went outside to give LC and Pete their scraps. Seeing them, the dogs made a happy noise. First they stood still and howled. Then they walked around and howled. Finally they got up on their hind legs and howled.

"Shame we don't speak Beagle," Papa said.

Tal did a half laugh through his nose as he divided the scraps for LC and Pete. He started to put some in Claudia's bowl but didn't because he knew the others would eat it as soon as they got through with their own.

"Think you might slip off and try your luck in the woods again this evening?" Papa said.

"I guess not," Tal said. "I'm pretty tired."

He expected to get teased about it, but Papa nodded. He drew on his pipe and blew a series of smoke rings. Tal tried that with his breath, which was visible but which wouldn't cooperate. Each attempt assembled itself into a feathery cloud.

"How you do those?" he said.

"Practice," Papa said. "It's all in the jaw."

LC and Pete began to whine when they finished eating.

"Don't even ask," Tal said. He pointed them to their house and they immediately obeyed. Once they were settled the only sound he could hear was the faint crackling the tobacco in Papa's pipe made when he pulled on it. Even Mama's chimes were still.

"You think Daddy wishes he was here, Papa?" he said.

"You bet he does," Papa said. "Nobody wants to be stuck way off somewhere separate from their family on Christmas Eve. It ain't right."

"Except for Claudia being gone, it's the most ain't-right thing I can think of," Tal said.

"It's up there," Papa said.

Tal watched Papa smoke. It was impossible to tell if he inhaled. Tal wondered if the smoke tasted as good as it smelled.

"You know what Mimi said about you doing that when you were bringing the dogs out here before we ate?" he said.

"She probably said she wants me to quit it for her Christmas present," Papa said.

"That was part of it," Tal said. "The rest was that she thinks the main reason you do it is to get her goat."

"Sounds like Mimi," Papa said.

"How sick are you, Papa?" Tal said.

The question surprised him almost as much as cussing in front of Daddy had the other morning. It just popped into his head and out of his mouth. He immediately regretted it—not because he thought he might have made Papa mad by asking but because he wasn't sure if he wanted the answer.

"That was stupid," he said. "Never mind."

"No, it's a fair question," Papa said. "All I can tell you is I've felt a whole lot better. Then again I don't reckon you'll find many men my age who wouldn't say the same thing. It ain't the pipe that's lined up against me now. It's all them son-of-a-bitching years. Seventy-three and counting. Seems impossible. I remember being your age like it was this morning."

"What seems impossible to me is you being afraid of the dark like you said this afternoon," Tal said. "Are you really?"

Papa looked toward the woods.

"Only when I think about it," he said.

The two of them stood together without saying anything else for quite a while. Then Papa knocked his pipe against the heel of his boot to empty the ashes. They hissed when they met the snow.

"Is Mimi going to get her present?" Tal said.

"I'm leaning that way just to see what she'll come up with to preach about next," Papa said.

"Fried food, probably," Tal said.

Papa laughed, then he coughed. But it didn't get away from him this time. He put his hand on Tal's upper arm and gave it a squeeze.

"Ready?" he said. "Santa Claus won't come unless you're asleep, I don't think."

"That's what they say," Tal said. "I know about Santa, Papa."

They headed toward the house.

"Know what about him," Papa said.

"That he's an idea," Tal said.

"Well, that may be true," Papa said. "But you just watch your sister in the morning if you think he ain't a good one."

Tal didn't know if he was sure about that.

"I appreciate the lantern, Papa," he said.

"Figured you might," Papa said. "A fellow needs him a light sometimes."

And now, everybody but Tal was asleep. Wide-awake, he took out one of his favorite books, *On the Ropes* by Otto Salassi. But his injured eye hurt and he had too much on his mind to concentrate. He read the same page three times without being able to remember any of it and set the book aside. He cut off his lamp. He thought about how different this part of Christmas Eve used to be back when he couldn't sleep because of what he believed. He couldn't do it now because of what he knew.

He felt lost and alone again. He tossed and turned, trying out different positions. Back. Right side. Left side. Stomach. All of them were equally uncomfortable. He propped his chin on his stacked fists. His thoughts jumped from Daddy and Claudia being away to howling wind and falling snow and shadows in the woods to Wink's struggle for breath under the toolshed. A lot could happen in ten years or in two days. He heard Papa coughing in the guest room. He wondered if that would get better or if whatever was wrong would just get worse and worse until it had Papa completely smothered the way the moccasin's poison had smothered Wink.

He glanced at the clock on his night table. It was almost midnight, the official beginning of Christmas Day. He wasn't looking forward to it. Too many things were out of order and there was nothing he could do about any of them. He covered his face with his pillow. He wished he still believed in the Santa Claus that was real, the one Jessie had set the snack out for, but he didn't. He couldn't. That part of him was gone. He'd outgrown it.

Eventually, he fell into a restless sleep and found himself

trying to make his way through knee-deep snow to the far side of a wide field where Daddy and Claudia were waiting for him. He couldn't get to them. He walked and walked without making any progress. He tried running, but the result was the same. He was still as far away from them as he'd been when he first started. He called to them. They didn't respond. They were no longer there. He awakened long enough to realize that they had vanished with the dream he'd been having.

Sometime later, during the wee hours of the morning, he opened his eyes. He was fully awake, roused by something. He wasn't sure what. He listened for a moment. Nothing. Then he heard LC and Pete. They had been barking but stopped when he woke up. This time they didn't stop. He went to his window. The glass was fogged over. He wiped it off with his hand.

It was too dark for him to be certain, but he thought he saw movement in shadows beyond the yard lamp. His heart began to pound. What if somebody had come to steal LC and Pete? He didn't have time to wake Papa because by then it might be too late. He wasn't sure what to do, but he knew that he needed to do something right away.

He slipped on his socks and moved quickly through the

house. He could hardly breathe when he got to the back door. He opened it just enough to peer out. The dogs were no longer barking, but somebody was definitely in the pen with them. There was no question about that. Tal clearly saw a figure just inside the gate, which was open. He was squatted down like a catcher, his back to the house. He remained in that position for a moment, then he stood and turned and was gone.

Tal gasped. He had caught just enough of a glimpse of the figure before it disappeared to register the red suit. Surely his eyes were playing tricks on him. Or maybe he was dreaming. But he couldn't be. His feet were chilled to the point of hurting. He was awake, all right. He just wasn't sure that he'd actually seen what he thought he had.

He opened the door a little wider and strained his ears, trying to hear somebody crunching through the snow. Except for his own breathing, the night was silent. He steadied himself.

"Hey!" he said. "Who's there?"

Nobody was. At least nobody answered. He pulled on his boots but didn't waste time with his coat. He had to get to LC and Pete. He looked for footprints on the way. At first he saw only his and Papa's from earlier. Then, nearing the pen, he noticed another set that made a trail between there and the toolshed. If who made them was who Tal thought might have, the purpose of his visit wouldn't be to steal anything. It would be exactly the opposite.

The gate was shut and latched. Tal eased it open.

"LC?" he said. "Pete?"

When he saw the dogs move from the shadows he dropped to his knees and spread his arms. They rushed forward to greet him, three dark shapes against the snow. The smallest was in the lead. She jumped and he caught her. He felt the weight of her, the energy, the life. He heard the little bell on her collar. He rocked her from side to side and she licked one of his cold ears with her warm tongue while LC and Pete danced in joyful circles around them.

16

Breakfast that morning was a sight to behold. There were fried chicken breasts, blood sausage links, bacon, eggs cooked in the bacon grease, grits covered with butter, cathead biscuits and gravy, coffee for the grownups, and hot chocolate for Tal and Jessie.

"This is a joy, having us all here together," Mimi said.

"Y'all didn't seriously think I'd miss Christmas because of a little slush on the road, did you?" Daddy said.

"Not me," Jessie said.

"Good for you," Daddy said.

"It's a miracle they didn't just load y'all back out to the platform," Papa said.

"They wouldn't dare," Mama said.

"Not and have to pay us holiday overtime," Daddy said.

"They'd probably figured out a loophole," Papa said. "An act of God comes in handy for company bosses and insurance adjusters."

"Ain't that the truth," Daddy said. "The thing is, you can only play so many hands of cards in a motel room knowing your family's holding Christmas for you. About noon yesterday old Theron Hayes from up in Emerson said he had to get out of there. He called the state police and they said the roads were bad but passable if he had four-wheel, which he does. We checked out half an hour later. Theron, me, and Bobby Joe Burgess from Haughton."

"Slow going?" Papa said.

"Barely moving," Daddy said. "But moving. Rolled into Haughton to drop Bobby Joe off at three o'clock this morning. Thirteen hours. Took us another three and a half from there to here. I never saw anything like it. I figure Theron made Emerson in an hour. I hated to let him go on that last little bit by hisself, but he's young and he knows how to put away the coffee. He might go to sleep by New Year's Eve."

"What kind of four-wheel, Daddy?" Tal said.

"Theron's got him a Jeep set up for off the road,"

Daddy said. "Wouldn't have been no other way without the tires on that thing. It's like a tank."

Tal thought back over what all had happened during the past few hours. He was still in a daze. After discovering Claudia in the pen where she belonged, he rubbed her, LC, and Pete until the cold began to get him. Then, shivering badly, he'd gone inside and returned to bed. The next thing he knew, Jessie was waking him up and telling him that Daddy was home.

"He drove with a man from Arkansas," she said. "Claudia's home, too, Talmidge. Come on. It's Christmas."

She left the room before Tal could say anything. He knew she was telling the truth about Claudia, and there was no way she'd lie about Daddy.

He sat up and scratched his head, amazed by the way things could change on you without warning. Sometimes it was from good to bad, but other times it went a different way. Life was just a mystery, that's all. There was no way to figure it out. He put on his eye patch and joined his family in the front room.

"Look what Santa brought us, Tal," Jessie said.

Tal glanced at the unwrapped presents—a bicycle and a backpack for Jessie, a New Orleans Saints sweatshirt and a football with a kicking tee for him. He gave Jessie a thumbs-up. Then he turned his attention to Daddy, who was sitting beside Mama on the fireplace ledge.

"You're really here," he said.

He hugged Daddy as hard as he'd hugged Claudia when she came out to greet him.

"Tell me about that eye," Daddy said.

"He said he's early for Halloween," Jessie said.

"Quite a bit, I'd say," Daddy said.

Tal knew he couldn't lie to Daddy and get away with it any longer than it would take him to say the words. Mama had already cut him more slack than he deserved by not pressing the subject. Daddy would cut him none.

He looked at Papa, hoping to put off what was coming a little longer.

"Could be a fellow just needs to have him a secret once in a while," Papa said. "Makes him feel in charge of something for a change. Somebody tell Tal about Claudia."

"Claudia's home," Jessie said. "Somebody found her and brought her back. Tubby Sims."

Tubby Sims was a good friend of theirs who worked for the same company Daddy did.

"Tubby found her?" Tal said. "Where?"

Daddy studied Tal. He didn't seem quite willing to buy Papa's philosophy. Tal waited for him to decide. He was ready to tell the truth and get it over with if he had to. After that he'd take what came. The others were waiting, too. Tal wished one of them would say something to break the silence. He was about to go ahead and do it himself when Daddy began to nod his head the way he had when he was figuring out how to deal with Tal for cussing in front of him. Tal just wasn't sure what he was agreeing with himself about this time. It could be that he didn't like the new territory they were in, that he'd rather pull Tal back to where the only thing he was in charge of was following the rules grownups made for him. This turned out not to be the case at all.

"A long way from here," Daddy said. "Tub come stomping in about five minutes after Theron left from letting me out at the company shack. I didn't want him to drive me all the way out here. I was in there signing out a truck and here comes Tub. He said he'd been reading gauges and was at the Number Nine well when he spied a dog backed up in there beside the pump engine, high and dry and warm as a biscuit. He knew who she belonged to, of course. Said she trotted right up to him like she'd been expecting him all along. I didn't know she'd been gone all that time until I got here. Mama filled me in."

"What did he have on?" Tal said.

"Let's see," Daddy said. "Set of red coveralls, I believe."

"It must've been him I saw then," Tal said.

"Saw Tub?" Daddy said.

Tal told the story, starting with LC and Pete waking him up and finishing with them and Claudia rushing forward to greet him. He left out the part about what he thought when whoever was there stood and turned. Now that he knew it was only Tubby, the idea seemed ridiculous and embarrassing.

"Old Tub," Daddy said. "He saved the day."

"Can we open presents now?" Jessie said.

"That's what we're here for," Daddy said. "Who wants to be Santa Claus?"

"Me," Jessie said. "I don't even have to look at names."

"I think yours is on most of this haul anyway," Papa said. "You must've been extra good this year."

"I'm always extra good," Jessie said.

She passed out the packages, and everybody went to work on them. Mama collected bows in a Piggly Wiggly sack. The wrapping paper went into a plastic trash bag.

"Maybe you ought to put in a word for me, Jessie," Papa said. "I checked a while ago and didn't see any Cadillacs parked nearby."

Tal noticed that Papa looked refreshed and wondered if he felt that way or if he just wasn't tired yet. He also noticed that Jessie hardly paused to examine any of her presents before tearing into the next one.

"Know what, y'all?" she said. "Christmas is my best day."

"Mine too, honey," Mimi said. "I'll always be especially fond of this one because listen to what this card from Papa says. It says, 'Well, Merry Xmas and you win. I'm keeping the pipe but only to chew on. Love from me, Your Husband.' "

Tal, Jessie, Mama, and Daddy all clapped their hands when Mimi kissed Papa's forehead and thanked him.

"One good thing is he'll have better breath now, ain't that right, Mimi?" Jessie said.

"Why, I hadn't thought of that," Mimi said. "Let me see."

She kissed him again, this time on the mouth.

"Sweet as syrup," she said.

"Have mercy," Papa said.

Tal's final gift was a pair of insulated hiking boots. An envelope was inside one of them. He thought it would contain money, but there was only a card. The picture on the front of it showed an oil derrick decorated like a Christmas tree. Tal opened the card and read to himself, "These ought to keep your feet warm when you take the dogs out. Love, Daddy (Santa)."

"That's what you wanted, I believe," Daddy said. "I just hope you don't get to liking going out there by yourself too much. I'd sure miss being with you once in a while."

"Thanks, Daddy," Tal said. "I don't think you have to worry about that."

Now, at the breakfast table, Papa was nudging Tal with his elbow.

"Looks like your Christmas turned out about half decent after all," he said.

Tal took a bite of chicken and nodded.

"I wouldn't swear to it, Jessie," Daddy said. "But I think we might have saw a sleigh pass over us down around Alexandria."

"Santa," Jessie said. "I heard reindeers on our roof last night, y'all."

"Were they prancing and pawing?" Papa said.

"No," Jessie said. "They stood and waited like they're suppose to. I only heard them land."

"Santa does have him some well-behaved deer," Papa said.

"Nobody can fry chicken this good," Daddy said. "Which one of y'all did it?"

"I'll not tell," Mimi said.

"Secret chef, secret recipe," Mama said.

"Well, a team like that ought to open them up a café," Daddy said. "Then I could retire."

"I don't see how anybody could eat fried chicken vittles for breakfast," Jessie said. "That's dinner or supper ones."

"Fried chicken's anytime vittles," Daddy said.

"Shoot, I reckon," Papa said.

"Don't you have but one of those, Papa," Mimi said. "I ought to've baked yours."

Papa glanced at Tal and shook his head.

"A fellow could keel over just looking at a spread like this," he said.

"Don't look too hard then," Mimi said.

"The reindeer landed with a little bump," Jessie said. "I wanted to go look, but I was too scared."

"They have a way of doing that to you," Papa said. "I know a world of youngsters who've heard them but not a one that had the spine to go take a peek."

"I'm doing it next year," Jessie said. "It's my revolution."

"Resolution, Jess," Tal said.

"I hope you see your reindeer, sweetheart," Mimi said.

"I hope I see Rudolph," Jessie said. "With his nose."

"You really mean that, don't you," Tal said.

"I surely do," Jessie said. "You could come with me if you want to, Talmidge."

The look on her face caused something to happen inside of Tal. It was like warm water running through his system. He felt the sensation of being weightless, as if he might levitate. Jessie believed as hard as a person could believe. Last night, when he was unable to go to sleep, he'd longed to believe like that again but couldn't. He thought he'd lost the ability to. But he hadn't. He started getting it back when he saw the figure in the pen stand and turn. He believed because he had no choice. It wasn't just an idea he was looking at. So what if it turned out to be Tubby Sims and not Santa

Claus? That didn't matter anymore. It wasn't ridiculous and embarrassing. He finally understood what Mama had tried to say two years ago. After she told him the truth, he quit believing because he wanted to be able to leave something behind like his friends had. And that's what he'd done. But Mama was telling him that knowing something wasn't real the way you thought it was didn't mean you had to quit believing in it. What you had to do was change the way you believed in it. If you didn't, you lost more than it. You lost yourself.

Jessie was practically shining with happiness. There was no reason to feel sorry for her or jealous of her either. She had the best gift of all, and she was sitting there giving it to him without even knowing. Tal hoped he could help her keep it when the time came.

"I think I'd like that, Jess," he said. "I'll stay as long as you want."

"Let's stay all night," Jessie said. "We'll hide in the toolshed."

"We'll see," Mama said.

She gave Tal a pleased nod and he bowed his head, smiling.

"What about your truck, son?" Papa said.

"It's sitting down in Morgan City with a coat of snow on it," Daddy said. "I might take a day next week and pick it up. Somebody from up here's always running down there, so it wouldn't be a problem. But I may just let it sit. Haven't decided. One thing's sure. I'm going to see the boys down in Minden about a four-wheel-drive rig first chance I get."

"I just can't get over that little Claudia," Mimi said. "No wonder she never heard y'all calling. That well's way up yonder by the Hammontree place."

"A good two miles," Daddy said. "You could've been right on top of her hollering until your throats bled and not got her attention over the clatter of that engine. Thing sounds like a car backfiring. I just hope it didn't blow out her ears."

"What do you think took her so far?" Mama said.

"That we'll never know," Papa said. "I'd guess a deer. Shame we don't speak Beagle, ain't that right, Tal?"

This time, unlike the night before when he could only snort halfheartedly at the same line, Tal laughed out loud. Then, without really thinking about it, he took off the patch and laid it on the table.

"Hey, Jessie," he said. "Look here."

"My gracious, honey," Mimi said.

"What's the other guy look like?" Daddy said.

"There wasn't any other guy," Tal said. "It was just me. I did this to myself."

"How?" Jessie said.

"It's a secret," Tal said. "Like Papa told y'all."

The grin he wore was huge and genuine. He was feeling better than he had since the snow began to fall.

17

Tal was more nervous than he thought he'd be, but he had to do this. He couldn't decline or postpone it. The time had come for him to accept his present from Daddy and with it the challenge of returning to the woods by himself. He wore his new boots and carried his new lantern.

The clouds that made the woods so claustrophobic for the past two days had begun to break up by mid-afternoon. By dusk they remained only as a smear in the west, the remnants of a sunset Jessie called their attention to and they all watched together from the front yard. The six of them had stood there silent as the snow family she and Tal had made. After the sun was gone, Papa packed and threw a snowball at Tal, who retaliated with one of his own. The fight was gentle but spirited. Even Mimi participated.

"I haven't done this in years," she said.

"It ain't snowed in years," Papa said.

Tal got Daddy in the back and paid for it with one to the neck. The dogs ran among them, leaping at the balls of snow they threw. When they quit, Tal took the dogs to their pen and fed them. He closed the gate while they were still eating.

"Don't worry," he said. "This day ain't over yet. I'll be back in a little while."

Now that night had fallen the sky was completely clear. Daddy and Papa accompanied Tal to the pen. Above them floated a fingernail moon and all of the winter stars. Tal pretended he wasn't tense, but he was and the men knew it. Papa did for sure. He hadn't told Tal's secret, though. That was still locked up good and tight.

The dogs were waiting at their gate. They were fed, rested, and ready to go. When Tal released them they raced out into the yard, their noses to the snow. Daddy, Papa, and Tal moved toward the tree line and stopped. Papa took out his pipe. He put it between his teeth without loading it.

"You ought to throw that thing away, is what you ought to do," Daddy said.

"I'd feel naked," Papa said.

"Well, it's a step in the right direction," Daddy said. "I'll give you that. Call them up, Tal. This is as far as we're going."

Tal whistled, but his mouth was so dry that the sound was mostly breath. Papa removed his pipe and clicked his tongue. LC and Pete came immediately. Claudia briefly paused to look in the direction of the sound Papa made and went back to work. Her ears were fine.

"Yonder is one serious little hunter," Papa said.

"She's a champ," Daddy said. "Okay, Tal. Just lead them in and find yourself a spot, then wait to see what they run by you."

"And hope it ain't a bear," Papa said.

Tal shot him a look. Papa smiled, chewing the stem of his empty pipe.

"Highly unlikely since there ain't none out there," he said.

The dogs moved in and out of the light from Tal's lantern, whining as they searched the coated ground for a scent. Then—with a sudden, startling trail bawl that caused Tal's heart to hammer—Claudia flashed past them and disappeared into the trees. Answering, LC and Pete followed. Their three fine voices blended, bell-like, and the chase was on.

"I guess they were tired of lollygagging," Papa said. "What a sound."

"You're on your own now, Talmidge," Daddy said. "That's probably a rabbit. I saw a big one out here this afternoon. All you have to do is use your head and trust the dogs. They'll come back around directly."

Tal held the lantern up. For a long moment he stared past the screen of light into the dark woods, listening to the dogs as they moved steadily away.

"They're running, Tal," Daddy said. "Go on."

His voice seemed far off, partly because of the blood that was pounding in Tal's ears and partly because he was trying to focus every bit of his attention on the dogs. But he did register the comment and it was like a spur. He started forward.

The dogs had probably covered a hundred yards by the time he stepped into the woods. The rabbit, if that's what they were after, would turn sooner or later. Tal wanted to see it pass in the woods, not in the backyard of his house, so he walked quickly. His heart continued to labor, but it soon settled into a regular rhythm, still hard and strong but pushed now by something other than nervous adrenaline. He concentrated on the distant baying of the dogs, Claudia in the lead, and imagined himself connected to them by a long rope that kept him from straying off the path they'd taken. Pulled along by their music, he was able to disregard the shadows that surrounded him.

He worked his way through the trees until he reached the two-track where he'd become spooked two nights ago. He found the place where the animals had crossed, and examined their prints in the snow. The dogs' quarry was indeed a rabbit, maybe the one Daddy had seen earlier. Tal rested on one knee and marveled at the twin impressions its huge rear paws had left. Standing, he studied the curtain of trees before him. Cloaked by the snow, they appeared ghostly in the thin moonlight. He felt his fear tugging at him. Every nerve in his body seemed to catch fire, urging him to return to Daddy and Papa. He swallowed hard. He tried to calm himself, but he was losing the battle. Then he heard the dogs change direction, their voices more urgent. The rabbit had turned.

As the chase approached him, he remembered that Papa had said he was only afraid of the dark when he thought about it. Tal realized that he didn't mean this dark. He meant the kind of dark that nobody understands because all they know about it is that it's waiting. Papa was getting old and didn't feel well. He was afraid of that, so he didn't think about it. What he did was accept that it made him afraid and started from there. If you paused to think about being afraid of something, you'd spend all your time trying to avoid it. You wouldn't be able to do anything else. The only way to deal with fear was to ignore it because if you didn't it would follow you as far as you went.

Released by this knowledge, Tal relaxed. He was alone in the dark, but he wasn't going to let himself surrender to how afraid it made him. He was going to stay put. He was going to keep running the dogs all by himself.

The rabbit that streaked past him a few moments later was the biggest one he'd ever seen. It hit the two-track, bounded to the other side, and disappeared. Tal whistled, and when one by one the dogs entered the opening they obeyed his signal and quit the chase. Their job was done. They were breathing hard, pleased with themselves. Tal set his lantern down and stroked their backs, praising each of them in turn. Ignored and defeated, his fear retreated into the shadows. He knew it wasn't gone for good and never would be. He also knew he had it whipped for the time being. Looking at the starry sky, he drew a breath of cold air deep into his lungs. He closed his eyes to savor the fresh, clean taste of it.

Claudia's bark startled him. She had come upon another scent and was off to find out where it led, LC and Pete close behind. Alone again, Tal started to call them back but thought better of it. He listened to the wonderful song they were singing and hoped that Daddy and Papa were hearing it, too. He wished they were with him, not because he was afraid but because he knew at last what running the dogs was really all about. It was about being in a place you loved with people you loved. You talked and laughed and listened to those baying voices together. Doing it alone wasn't nearly as much fun.

Still, he was feeling as good about being in the woods as he ever had. He was also feeling good about himself, proud that he'd held his ground and pleased that things had gone the way they had. The world was a thoroughly strange and mysterious place, but sometimes it gave you just what you wanted it to and made you grateful you were in it.

Smiling, he picked up his lantern and walked along the two-track to where the dogs had reentered the trees. He paused briefly to mark their music, then he headed confidently in that direction. He hoped they ran for a long time because it was a beautiful night and he was in no hurry to leave the woods, no hurry at all.